**Here's wh**
**Gem**

"A saucy combination of romance and suspense that is simply irresistible."
- Chicago Tribune

"Stylish...nonstop action...guaranteed to keep chick lit and mystery fans happy!"
- Publishers' Weekly, starred review

"Smart, funny and snappy…the perfect beach read!"
- Fresh Fiction

"If you have not read these books, then you are really missing out on a fantastic experience, chock full of nail-biting adventure, plenty of hi-jinks, and hot, sizzling romance. Can it get any better than that?"
- Romance Reviews Today

"(A) breezy, fast-paced style, interesting characters, and story meant for the keeper shelf. 4 ½!"
- RT Book Reviews

# BOOKS BY GEMMA HALLIDAY

### High Heels Mysteries
Spying in High Heels
Killer in High Heels
Undercover in High Heels
Christmas in High Heels
(short story)
Alibi in High Heels
Mayhem in High Heels
Honeymoon in High Heels
(short story)
Sweetheart in High Heels
(short story)
Fearless in High Heels
Danger in High Heels

### Hollywood Headlines Mysteries
Hollywood Scandals
Hollywood Secrets
Hollywood Confessions
Twelve's Drummer Dying
(holiday short story)

### Jamie Bond Mysteries
Unbreakable Bond
Secret Bond
Bond Bombshell
(short story)

### Tahoe Tessie Mysteries
Luck Be A Lady

### Young Adult Books
Deadly Cool
Social Suicide

### Other Works
Play Nice
Viva Las Vegas
A High Heels Haunting
Watching You (short story)
Confessions of a Bombshell
Bandit (short story)

# BOOKS BY JENNIFER FISCHETTO

### Disturbia Diaries Mysteries
I Spy Dead People

### Jamie Bond Mysteries
Unbreakable Bond
Secret Bond

# SECRET BOND

GEMMA HALLIDAY

AND

JENNIFER FISCHETTO

To all the readers who enjoyed *Unbreakable Bond*, thank you. This book wouldn't be possible without you.

~ Jenn

For Jackson, a great critique partner, a fantastic person to brainstorm with, and a nice bit of eye candy too.

~Gemma

# CHAPTER ONE

─────

"Roll up your window."

"It's 100 degrees outside."

"They're tinted. Less chance of someone seeing you."

I shot Derek a dirty look but complied, rolling up the window. Then I took off my jacket in an attempt to feel less like a roast pig as I shifted in my seat, peeling my thighs off the hot vinyl.

"That's better." Derek leaned back and put a pair of binoculars back up to his eyes, training them on the pink, stucco covered motel across the street again.

"I don't think he's coming," I said, fanning myself with an AARP brochure I'd found stuck between the seats of Derek's Bonneville.

"Oh, he's coming. You just gotta be patient, kid."

Patience was something I was woefully short on today. Usually I did stakeouts on my own. Or with one of my associates from the Bond Agency. But today Derek had insisted on riding along. I'd like to think it was just boredom and the restless heat wave that had recently hit Los Angeles and not that he didn't trust me to do the job right.

I'd like to think that, but I didn't really.

Derek Bond was a licensed PI, sixty-three years old—though his libido was perpetually stuck at sixteen—and feared by cheating husbands everywhere. Not because Derek was apt to sleep with their distraught wives, though I couldn't promise that hadn't happened on occasion, but because no matter who they were, how careful they were, or how slick they thought they were being, Derek would always catch them in the act—pants around the ankles, prostitute half naked, pre-nup busted to pieces. The Bond Agency had been synonymous with a quick and easy divorce for women all over L.A. for years.

That is until one of those cheating husbands had been upset enough to shoot Derek while on a stakeout at a seedy motel in a North Hollywood neighborhood not a whole lot unlike the one we were in now. After the shooting, Derek had been forced into early retirement, prescribed to take it easy on his weakened heart. That's when he'd reluctantly handed the reins of the Bond Agency over to his only child.

Me, Jamie Bond. Or as my father, ever hopeful that I'd come out a bouncing baby boy and a chip off the old block, had legally named me: James Bond. I'd spent the last twenty-nine years of my life trying to forgive him for that.

I'd honestly never wanted to be a PI myself. I'd grown up doing my homework in the back of this very same Bonneville on stake-outs very much like this one, which had given me more than enough of a taste of the domestic espionage game. Me—I'd dreamed of being a runway model. Which, at age fifteen, is exactly what I'd done, spending my late-teens and early-twenties strutting down the catwalks of Milan, Paris, and New York. A far cry from the faded sweatbox I was now seated in. But the truth was that when Derek got shot, my world changed forever. Suddenly, he needed me in a way I never thought possible. Besides, I wasn't getting any younger at the time (At twenty-six I'd been a dinosaur in model years.), and I did know the PI business inside and out. So, I'd taken over the reins and been the "Bond" in the agency ever since.

Not that it kept Derek from still sticking his nose into every aspect of it.

"How old did you say this guy was?" Derek asked from behind his binoculars.

"Forty-seven," I answered.

"And the chick he's banging?"

I winced at his less than PC choice of words. "The *woman* he's been *seeing* is twenty-one. But," I added, "I don't think they're showing today. It's too hot for adultery."

Derek shook his head. "Trust me. He's showing. A young piece of tail like that…"

Thankfully he trailed off and I didn't have to hear his thoughts on twenty-something "tail."

"I've got about ten more minutes in me," I warned him, feeling sweat trickle down my back, soaking the pink, silk tank I'd thrown on this morning. "Then I'm gonna start melting from the inside out."

Derek grunted in response.

"I'm serious, old man."

He ignored me. "How much is his wife paying you?" he asked instead, reaching into the center console and popping a piece of gum into his mouth. Watermelon flavored, if the scent hitting my nostrils was any indication.

"The usual."

"Which is?"

"None of your business."

Derek pulled the binoculars away from his eyes just long enough to shoot me a dirty look. "You're a tough one, Bond." Then he blew a big pink bubble my way.

I resisted the urge to pop it. Mostly because I didn't want to ruin my manicure.

"If you must know, I gave her a discount."

"How much?"

"On contingency," I muttered under my breath.

"Jesus, James. A charity case? Really?" He didn't look amused.

"Look, she was desperate. He's got all their money tied up. The only way she could afford to pay us was if we could get the goods on her ex-husband-to-be."

Derek shook his head at me. "I thought I trained you better than that, kid. Payment up front."

"We're fine. She'll pay. As soon as we catch the bastard."

"Speaking of whom…" Derek grinned, pointing out his smudged windshield.

Across the street, a BMW pulled up to the motel's parking lot. A guy with salt-and-pepper hair wearing a pressed pair of slacks got out, walked around to the passenger side, then opened the door for a brunette in Daisy-dukes who looked young enough to be his daughter.

"What did I tell you?" Derek asked, turning to me with a satisfied grin.

I shook my head. "I hate it when you're right." I grabbed my camera and popped off a couple of shots of the happy couple entering a room on the ground floor.

"Yeah, but you love catching your mark," Derek said.

Dammit, the old man was right again.

* * *

"Hit me with new business," I said the following morning, walking through the doors to the Bond Agency conference room. My three faithful employees greeted me: a "Morning, boss," from the first two and a Starbucks Caramel Macchiato from the third. I loved my girls.

After a very successful afternoon in No Ho catching our sunny day adulterer, I'd celebrated by first dropping Derek back at his boat, which served as his permanent residence these days, then treating myself to a steak dinner, a glass of 1994 merlot, and a hot bubble bath. All of which had put me in an excellent mood this morning as I held my coffee in one hand and my cell in the other, pulling up my schedule for the day.

"Three messages," Maya, my receptionist, told me, sliding three pieces of pink notepaper across the polished wood table at me. "One from Mrs. Mueller, wondering how it went with Mr. Mueller yesterday."

"Fabulously," I answered, picturing the eight-by-tens we'd taken of him and the leggy brunette.

"The second was Aiden." Maya paused, sending me a meaningful glance. "Wanting to know if you are free this evening."

I raised an eyebrow. Aiden Prince was the new L.A. County Assistant District Attorney: charming, smart, and blessed with classic good looks that had my friends dubbing him ADA Ken Doll. His suits were Brook Brothers, his aftershave was subtle, and his morals were unshakable. His wife had died of cancer a year ago, prompting him to leave his native Kansas City and start over on the west coast. I'd met Aiden a few months ago on a case, and our relationship was currently in that indefinable grey area. To call him a boyfriend would be seriously jumping the gun. To say he was just a friend was understating it a bit. But at the sound of his name, I couldn't help a fluttery feeling in the pit of my stomach.

"I hope you told him I had to check my schedule?" I said. Hey, I had to play just a little hard-to-get.

Maya nodded. "I told him I wasn't sure you were free and that you'd call him back."

"Perfect." I nodded, sitting down in a leather chair at the end of the table. "And the third call?"

"New case," Sam jumped in.

Samantha Cross was my right hand woman when it came to undercover work. She had honey mocha skin, legs that went on forever, and was a former winner of *America's New Hot Model.* She was also an expert with firearms, thanks to a military brat upbringing, and a struggling single mom who never balked at working overtime to bust a guy who really deserved it.

"Music to my ears," I responded. "Who?"

"Danielle Martin," Sam said, reading from a printout in her hand. "She owns an antique shop and thinks her husband is playing around on her. She wants proof before filing divorce papers."

I nodded. Standard issue.

"But there's a twist," the girl seated next to Sam added. Caleigh Presley, the complete polar opposite of Sam. Sweet as thick molasses, she was the quintessential southern girl next door. Blonde, blue-eyed, and bubblier than a Coke, Caleigh claimed she was a distant cousin to the one and only Elvis. She was also an excellent computer hacker, thanks to spending all of her childhood's sultry southern summers in the air conditioned bliss of her parents' library. Skills that had come in handy on more than one occasion.

"I love a twist," I told her, leaning back in my chair. "Hit me."

"He's a nudist."

I blinked at her, not sure I'd heard right. "Excuse me?"

"Mr. Martin…" Caleigh looked down to check her notes. "…David Martin, that is, is a nudist."

"As in, he doesn't wear any clothes," Sam hammered home.

"Ever?" I asked, picturing the guy walking down Hollywood Boulevard au naturel.

Sam shook her head. "No, he wears clothes in public. But he spends a few days a month at a nudist colony in Big Bear. That's where the wife thinks the husband is stepping out on her."

"He claims," Caleigh jumped in, "that being a nudist is about being—and I quote from the wife—'unencumbered by the societal judgments and confines of our outer shells to be one with nature.'"

"And the wife buys this?" I asked.

Sam shook her head. "She thinks it's about being one with naked women."

I was inclined to agree with the wife.

"She wants us to tail him this week and see what he's really up to," Sam added.

"Wait." I held up a hand. "Tail him at the nudist colony?"

Caleigh nodded, her eyes twinkling with something akin to glee. "Uh-huh."

"Which means we're going to have to go undercover..."

"Naked," Caleigh finished for me, grinning from ear to ear. "Imagine all the hot naked guys we're going to see on this one. I can't wait." She was fairly bouncing in her seat with excitement.

Oh, boy. This was going to be interesting.

* * *

Aiden looked across the table at me and almost choked on his sip of chardonnay. "You're going to a nudist colony?"

I shot him a look. "Don't do that."

"Do what?"

"Look at me like that. Like you're imagining me naked right now."

Aiden grinned, setting his glass down. "You know, it's kind of impossible not to."

I sighed. "Would I be wrong to send Sam and Caleigh on their own with this one?"

"Come on. Don't tell me you're a prude, Jamie," Aiden teased.

I snorted. "Hardly. I did four Victoria's Secret catalogues."

"Okay, now I'm *really* imagining you naked."

I swatted his arm from across the table.

We were at Chianti's Italian Restaurant off Melrose, sharing a bottle of very nice wine, ordering very small appetizers, and enjoying the very dim lighting and romantic atmosphere. I was starting to mellow from the wine, and certain parts of my body were starting to get keyed up from the flirtatious tone in Aiden's voice. It wasn't an altogether unpleasant combo.

"So, what did you want to talk to me about tonight?" I asked, doing an obvious subject change. When I'd called Aiden back that morning, he'd said there was something he wanted to discuss with me at dinner. I'd been just the slightest bit disappointed that he'd had an agenda other than wooing me into bed, but I'd agreed to meet anyway, hoping maybe an agenda *and* wooing were on his mind.

"Right." Aiden shifted in his seat, his demeanor going from flirtatious to the official business mode I'd seen him adopt in the courtroom. "It's about a case I'm trying."

I cocked an eyebrow his way. "Oh?"

"It involves a former police officer. Jack Brady. You may have heard of the case?"

I nodded. I was no CNN devotee, but it was hard not to hear about the Brady case. Jack Brady had been a career officer of the LAPD until he'd allegedly killed a man in cold blood three years ago. He was currently being tried for the murder, which had all of L.A. on riot alert due to the tenuous relationship between the LAPD and the people of Los Angeles.

"He killed an attorney, right?" I asked, picking up my own glass and taking a sip.

"Correct. Edward Bernstein. Brady tried to pass it off as a routine shooting, saying the attorney pulled a weapon on him."

"I'm guessing he didn't?"

"We have no evidence to support Brady's claim," Aiden said, using the typically vague lawyer speak I'd come to expect from him.

"The case sounds pretty cut and dried," I observed.

Aiden nodded. "It is. We have ample evidence of corruption on Brady's part. I'm confident we'll get a conviction on this one." He picked up a breadstick from the basket in the center of the table, absently pulling off a crusty end. "But there was something that came up in the discovery process."

"Oh?" I asked again, swirling my wine.

"The gun Brady used to shoot his victim." Aiden paused, still focusing on his bread, not looking up, his jaw visibly tense.

I set the wine glass down. "What is it?"

He cleared his throat, eyes avoiding mine. "As we were preparing the forensic evidence for the trial, we ran the gun through the system again, just to be thorough."

"And?" I asked, a niggle of dread starting to form in my stomach. He still wouldn't look at me.

"And we found a match to the bullet striations. Turns out the same gun was used in a previous crime."

"You're killing me here, Aiden. Spit it out. What does this have to do with me?"

Aiden blew out a breath, finally looking up, and sent a weak smile my way. "I should have known I couldn't dance around it with you."

"Dance around what? What crime was the gun used in?" I asked, even though that dread, growing into a hard ball now, gave me a sneaking feeling I already knew.

"A shooting. Three years ago." Aiden leaned in. "Your dad, Jamie. Brady's gun was the same weapon that was used to shoot Derek."

# CHAPTER TWO

———

I'd been on location in the south of France. It was a shoot for *Italian Vogue*, one which my agent, Maurcess DeLine, had been giddy to book for me. Couture dresses, European elegance, top photographers, including my best friend, Danny Flynn, and a never-ending river of champagne that flowed throughout our days.

We'd been up drinking all night, me and the two other models booked on the shoot, in our suite at the Champ de Marie hotel. Danny was drunk, entangled with a redheaded model, while I'd been giggling and acting like a tipsy fool with a French photographer who spoke zero English but had mastered the universal art of body language. Dawn was just starting to peek over the clay-tiled rooftops outside our balcony when the suite's phone rang. Danny answered, and I watched his expression from across the room, going from mellow-with-redhead-and-booze to stark white.

"Jamie?" he'd said, his voice tight, his Adam's apple bobbing up and down. Something was wrong. Really wrong.

And then he'd said the words. "It's Derek."

As I'd taken the phone from him and listened to a nurse on the other end say things like "tissue damage", "ICU", and "unstable condition," my entire childhood had flashed before my eyes. As much as I might have resented Derek's brand of parenting, after Mom died, he was all I had left.

I'd gotten on the first flight home, arriving jet lagged and puffy-eyed at the hospital where I had hardly recognized him. Tubes spilled out of his arms, nose, and mouth. A machine breathed for him, another feeding him, and a third sending medication to his body to keep his heart pumping. The bullet had hit him in the chest, miraculously bypassing his heart and major arteries as it lodged into his shoulder. He'd been lucky. An inch to the left, and he would have been dead on arrival. As it was, the doctors had given him a fifty-fifty chance. I should have known then that Derek was too stubborn to die. But I hadn't. I'd just known that as much as my father was a pain in the ass, I'd wanted him to live.

And I'd wanted to kill the person who'd done that to him.

"Are you saying that Brady shot my father?" I asked Aiden, the words sounding oddly disconnected even to my own ears, almost as if I was listening to someone else say them.

Aiden sighed, fiddling with his breadstick some more. "No. I'm saying the same gun was used to shoot your father."

"Where is the gun now?" I asked, my wineglass forgotten.

"In evidence. Same place it's been since they arrested Brady."

"Was it Brady's service revolver?"

"No. It was an unregistered street weapon. 9mm."

"So it could have belonged to anyone? I mean, Brady could have gotten it from the guy who shot Derek before he shot the attorney."

Aiden nodded. "That's possible."

"Or Brady could have done both shootings himself."

"That's possible as well."

He wasn't giving me much. But I knew one thing was for sure.

A new case had just jumped to the top of my priority list.

\* \* \*

As soon as I got home, I logged into the agency's remote files and pulled up our case notes on Derek's shooting. There weren't a lot. Derek had, obviously, been laid up, and I'd yet to take on the role of any sort of investigator. Still, there were police reports and a few random thoughts Derek had typed up after the fact.

Derek had always believed that it was the husband he'd been tailing that night who'd shot him. Benson Booker. It had been a typical adultery case; the Bookers were married ten years, three kids, the husband suspected of seeking "professional company" with Russian hookers. One night Derek was staking out a motel in NoHo where Booker was thought to meet with his ladies, in hopes he'd show. Instead, a masked man had come up to Derek's driver's side window and shot him. Didn't say a word, didn't ask for money, just shot him, point blank. Then he took off, leaving Derek for dead.

Unfortunately there had never been any hard evidence in the case. A bullet pulled from Derek's shoulder had been the sole physical evidence left at the scene. Not enough to implicate anyone in particular.

Until now.

I stared at the screen in front of me. Could it be that Brady had shot my father? Had Booker and Brady known each other? Had Booker hired the dirty cop to do the deed for him? Or did this have nothing to do with Booker at all. Had Brady had something personal against Derek?

I grabbed my cell, keying in Derek's number. Five rings in, I got voicemail.

"Call me back," I told his machine. "We need to talk."

\* \* \*

I spent the night tossing and turning, reliving those horrible moments in the hospital, watching Derek flirt with the big stake-out in the sky. I awoke still tired, achy, and wanting answers.

I stumbled into the bathroom and frowned at the bags under my eyes in the mirror, adding extra mascara to combat their appearance, then dressed in my usual uniform of a pencil skirt, heels, silk tank and loose linen jacket. It was as professional as I got without roasting in the heat. I grabbed my Glock 27, briefcase, and purse, heading for the elevator, then crossed the already sizzling macadam parking lot to my red roadster. I didn't have kids, didn't have a pet, and had no intentions of purchasing a bungalow in the burbs anytime soon. My disposable income was all sports car.

Twenty traffic filled minutes later, I was pushing my way through the frosted glass doors of the agency, embellished with the single word "Bond" in bold, black letters. The lobby was small, but tastefully decorated by Maya's hand. Two black, leather chairs along one wall, a reception desk on the other, and framed modern art on the walls. A short carpeted hallway opened up to my office on the right and a conference room done in light, modern colors and dark woods on the left.

Maya was at the reception desk, manning phones, and I spied Caleigh and Sam already at the conference table, nursing a couple of coffees. As soon as I walked into the room, Caleigh placed a third cup in my hand.

"Bless you," I told her, taking a grateful sip.

"Late night?" Sam asked.

I nodded. "Sort of." I hesitated to drag the girls into what Aiden had told me. It wasn't technically an agency case, and it was definitely personal.

I'd left Derek two more voicemails this morning, though I didn't actually expect to hear from him until after noon. One of the perks of being a retiree is that the man slept ten hours a day.

"Late night sounds promising," Caleigh said, leaning both elbows on the table. "Did you and Aiden finally seal the deal?"

I blinked at her. "Excuse me?"

"You did have a date with the ADA last night, right?" Caleigh prompted.

"Oh. Yeah. Right."

"So…come on, deets!" she demanded.

Honestly, there were precious few to relay. After his revelation, we'd both picked at our meals, then I'd passed on tiramisu and headed home right after, anxious to look at our case files. Okay, there had been a very brief hug and a kiss on the cheek from Aiden, but it was hardly the passionate "late night" I was sure Caleigh envisioned.

"No deets to give. It was dinner," I said, sitting in a leather chair. "What's on the agenda for today?"

Caleigh opened her mouth to protest, but Sam nudged her under the table, shooting her a look that clearly said to drop it if she valued her job. Sam was a smart girl.

As if on cue, Maya walked through the conference room door, flicking her fingers across her tablet. "No new business this morning," she informed the room. "But Mrs. Mueller will be in this afternoon to pick up the photos of her husband and his fling at the motel."

"Fab."

"And," Caleigh interjected, "we have Martin today."

"Martin?" I asked, the caffeine slow to penetrate my brain this morning.

"The nudist!" There was Caleigh's giddy face again.

I groaned. I'd forgotten all about him. "Please tell me that you two are working this one without me?" I asked.

Sam shook her head. "Sorry, boss. Mrs. Martin requested you specifically."

"Swell."

"But don't worry," Sam said. "I talked to Mrs. Martin, and she said not everyone at the resort goes full monty all the time."

"Sometimes they wear cover-ups. You know, to protect themselves from the sun," Caleigh added. "Which Sam bought for us."

Thank God for small favors.

"Fine. Let's get this over with," I said.

Famous last words.

Half an hour later Caleigh, Sam and I had all donned loose cover-ups that looked like skimpy wrap dresses, leather sandals, and sunglasses, and I was following Sam's Cherokee up the 330 in my roadster, heading toward the lake.

The Bare Necessities nudist colony was located in Big Bear, a recreation area just east of Los Angeles, known for its sparkling blue lake in the summer and world class ski slopes in the winter. Only an hour and a half drive from the office, the wall to wall concrete gave way here to towering pine trees and an odd scent that Caleigh informed me was called "fresh air". Communities of vacation retreats, small cabins, and campgrounds dotted the landscape, and the roads wound increasingly higher up the mountain, growing increasingly more narrow before leading us to a carved wooden sign proclaiming we'd found a "natural paradise" at the colony. I followed Sam onto the paved road, which led to a resort that looked like any other ski resort in the area. Of course, at this time of year snow was noticeably absent, replaced by thick, dry grasses and blazing sunshine. Though, thankfully, at this elevation the heat wasn't quite as intense as in the valley.

We parked, and Sam checked the three of us in, using the reservation number Maya had secured the day before. We were booked for two nights—exactly the same as Mr. Martin. I hoped it would be enough to catch the guy in the act.

After getting our room number, we drove around the back of the resort, pulling into parking slots near the room.

"This is going to be so fun," Caleigh squealed, stepping from Sam's car, eyes already scanning the walkway for hot, naked men.

"Let's focus, shall we?" I suggested.

"Right. Martin's wife said he likes to hang out near the pool," Sam offered.

"Perfect! Let's hit the pool!" Caleigh said, clapping her hands.

I wished I could share her enthusiasm as we walked toward the center of the complex.

But as soon as we hit the courtyard, I felt my jaw drop open. The setting was beautiful, the sparkling water surrounded by rocks made it look like the chlorinated pool had naturally sprung up in the middle of the pine groves. Trees flanked the area, green and fragrant, towering over the scene. Chaise lounges lined the poolside, and two private cabanas sat off to the right. A wooden bar sat on the other side, manned by a bartender that was, at least from the waist up above, totally nude. As were all of the resort patrons, lounging on their chaises. I counted ten people and only one bikini bottom.

And, unlike the visions Aiden was having last night, not all of them could qualify as supermodels. Or even non-super models. In fact, the average age of the patrons seemed to be somewhere in the mid-fifties, and I could easily see what a lifetime of nude sunbathing had done to their skin. Wrinkling, leathery, sagging in all the wrong places. While I was usually the last person to judge another based on the size or shape of their body, I was having a hard time looking away from the train wreck of human flesh.

"Where are the hot guys?" Caleigh asked, her voice high.

"Maybe they hide them in another part of the resort," I whispered back.

"I changed my mind," Caleigh said, swallowing hard. "I don't think this is going to be all that fun after all."

After asking around, we found Mr. Martin was one of the sunbathers near the end of the line of loungers. He was a pale, freckled redhead, applying copious amounts of sunscreen to his arms. (I prayed we got out of here before other parts of him needed sun screened!) Sam and I hung back, sending Caleigh in first. I could see her trying to avert her eyes and stare at anything other than his freckled little Mr. Martin as she engaged him in conversation.

Sam and I watched, taking up spots at the bar beside the pool and ordering a pair of margaritas from the bartender who was, in fact, nude from the waist down as well. I'll admit, I peeked behind the bar to check.

He gestured to my cover-up as he handed my drink to me. "First timer to the resort?"

"Uh, yeah."

He winked. "I thought so. I can always spot nudity virgins."

Sam choked a little on her margarita next to me, stifling a laugh.

"Don't worry," he said. "You'll get more comfortable. Everyone starts out a bit shy."

I sent him a wan smile. "Oh, I'm sure I'll be strutting my nude self in no time."

"I can't wait for that," he said, giving me another wink.

I think I heard Sam snort next to me as he turned away.

"Please let Mr. Martin be a quickie," I mumbled.

"Well, look at it this way—he's already got his clothes off. That's gotta save some time," Sam joked.

I grinned at her. "Let's hope."

"Speaking of getting naked…" Sam said. "What really happened with Aiden last night?"

I shrugged. "Like I said. Nothing."

"I thought you were hot on him?" Sam eyed me.

"I am. Sort of. I guess. I don't know. I mean, we'll see."

"Well, that was definite."

I shot her a look. "Aiden is fine. I just…" I trailed off, not sure how personal I wanted to get here.

"You're holding out on me," she said, reading my mind.

"Okay, he told me something. About a case he's trying. It was… surprising. It kinda shook me."

"Want to share?" Sam asked.

I paused. Then shook my head. "Not yet."

"Fair enough," Sam said, taking a sip of her drink. "I'm here if you do."

I sipped, too, grateful she wasn't pressing it.

We sat in silence, both trying to avert our eyes from the flabby, sagging, and generally horrifying sights of the human body in various forms as more patrons filled the pool area in the early afternoon sunshine.

Finally Caleigh came jogging back toward us.

"Any luck?" I asked.

She shrugged. "He didn't proposition me, but…" She paused. Her face turned red. And she lowered her voice. "But without pants, it was pretty hard for him to disguise his interest."

I snorted my margarita, feeling lime juice go up my nose. "Well, that's a start."

# CHAPTER THREE

———

I left Sam and Caleigh in the room to strategize their next attempt at Martin. I was confident they could carry on without me for a few hours. At least until the "Bare Boogie" dance that night in the recreation hall that the resort brochure had promised. I think I'd seen Caleigh visibly shudder when she'd read it.

Me—I had other things to look into. I drove back to the office, cranking the AC the entire way. I entered the reception area, still wearing my loose cover-up that, while it had seemed downright prudish at the nudist colony, here in clothing-not-optional land was barely covering my important parts.

A fact that my best friend Danny let me know as soon as I walked in the door.

"Hell-o, skin," he said, a toothy grin spreading across his face as he rocked back on his heels. "I'm suddenly seeing the upside of the heat wave."

"Contain yourself. It's for an assignment," I said, trying in vain to make the cover-up cover more up.

"Whatever it is, I'm loving this assignment," he said, following me into my office.

"Nudist colony," I replied.

That stopped Danny in his tracks, his eyes getting that same giddy, glazed look that Caleigh's had at first. "And you didn't call me? I'm hurt, Bond. Truly hurt."

I shook my head.

Danny Flynn was tall, spent enough time at the gym that he liked to show it off, and had a warm outdoor tan and sun-streaks in his light brown hair year round. He was older than I was by a few years, but the only betrayals of his age were fine laugh lines at the corners of his eyes, which somehow only added to his boyish charm instead of detracting from it. His eyes were somewhere between a sea green and a pale blue depending on his mood, and he was a swimsuit photographer who had a bad habit of taking his work home with him. I'd met Danny on my first modeling shoot, when I was fifteen and feeling downright gangly and awkward in my bikini with a dozen lights blaring at me. Danny had immediately stepped into the big brother role, putting me at ease and showing me how to make my skinny limbs look like graceful art on camera.

Over the years, Danny had morphed from big brother to best friend, but there were times recently when I'd sworn there was an emotion that read deeper than friendship lurking behind his pale eyes. I wasn't quite sure how I felt about that yet.

"Down, boy," I told him, grabbing my pencil skirt and tank from the hangers on the back of my door. "It's not all it's cracked up to be. You ever see a naked forty-something mother of four with C-section scars and stretchmarks up close?"

Danny paused, having to think about that one. "I don't think so."

"I have. It's not pretty."

"Hmm. I'll take your word for it," he said, though I could still see visions of nude hotties dancing in his eyes.

"Turn around," I instructed, pulling my pencil skirt on under my cover-up.

Danny did as told, turning his back to me. "So...you and the girls going in the buff?"

"Not if I can help it. This cover-up is as far as I want to go," I said, dropping the item in question and slipping my tank over my head.

"Bummer."

I swatted his backside. "You are incorrigible."

"Hey, I have a healthy interest in the female form." He paused. "Particularly yours."

I rolled my eyes at his back, stepping back into my pumps. "Flattery will get you nowhere, pal."

"Well, you're no fun. Surely you girls need a little back-up on this case?"

"I tell you what," I said, strapping my Glock back on. "I'm going back up to the resort tonight. You can ride shotgun if you want."

"Oh, I want," Danny said, turning around. His eyes zeroed in on my cleavage area as if already imaging the region in the buff.

I crossed my arms over my chest. "Okay, but when your corneas are scarred for life by the parade of unsightly nudists, don't say I didn't warn you."

Danny just grinned. "I'll take my chances."

"Now, if you'll excuse me," I said, grabbing my purse and heading for the door again.

"Where you off to?" he asked. "I was hoping we could do lunch."

"Sorry, rain check," I told him. "I've got to go see a man about a gun."

\* \* \*

Derek lived on the humorously named *Black Pearl*, a cabin cruiser perpetually docked in Maria Del Rey. It wasn't docked in the ritziest marina in the L.A. area, but even among the modest crafts, Derek's old clunker looked like it was about to sink at any second. It was dented, discolored, and painted different colors in different places, just depending on what paint happened to be on sale that day. The deck sported a couple of rusted patio chairs and a table, the interior modestly furnished in eighties cast-offs. It held a bedroom, with a bathroom that was just big enough to turn around in, a pair of bunks in the mid cabin next to a storage closet, and a small galley that served as his kitchen. I stepped on board, my heels clacking against the uneven wooden beams and took a minute to let my balance catch up with the sway of the boat before proceeding below deck.

"Knock, knock," I said as I descended the stairway, banging a fist on the entryway to the galley.

A few resulting rustling sounds greeted me from the bedroom.

"You here, Derek?" I asked. The kitchen counter held the remnants of last night's dinner—frozen pizza, an empty six pack of Budweiser, and a half eaten apple pie. I felt an eyebrow raise. The pie was interesting. I could no sooner imagine Derek baking than I could myself drinking domestic from a can.

"I'm giving you a five count, then I'm coming in," I yelled. An idle threat. I'd seen enough naked people today to last a lifetime. The last thing I wanted to walk in on was Derek sleeping in the buff.

"I'm up," I heard from the back in an almost human growl.

I looked down at my watch. It was past two.

A minute later, Derek emerged, clad in a pair of boxers and an L.A. Dodgers T-shirt with a suspicious looking yellow stain on the front. "What are you doing here, kid?" he asked, stumbling to a coffee pot in the corner.

"I wanted to talk. You didn't get my messages?"

"Been busy," he growled, pulling a can of Folgers from the cupboard.

I was about to ask if sleeping qualified as busy, when I heard a second set of rustling sounds from the bedroom. A bleached blonde wearing an oversized T-shirt and a bad case of bed head emerged, swaying in the doorway like she had a hell of hangover. "Coffee. Must have coffee," she croaked out through a pack-a-day cough.

I raised an eyebrow at Derek. "Ah. I see. Busy."

"James, you know Elaine," Derek said.

I did. Sort of. I'd met her a couple of times, though I had to admit I hadn't made an effort to get to know her. Derek went through women like I went through handbags. Just when one started to get comfortable, he moved on to the next. Elaine had been flavor of the moment for over a month now. Her shelf life was near expiration if Derek's track record was any indication.

"Good morning," I said, giving her a little wave.

To her credit, she attempted a smile in my direction before grabbing a coffee mug.

"Can we go up top?" I asked Derek as he poured himself a cup. "I'd like to talk to you in private."

Elaine waved in my direction. "Don't mind me. I gotta get to work anyway," she mumbled, taking her steamy mug of black coffee back to the bedroom, only sloshing a little on the floor in her unsteady wake.

I gestured to her retreating back. "Careful, Derek. She's becoming a regular."

He grinned, sitting at the small galley table, some of the growl coming out of his voice as the coffee worked its magic. "That's not all bad. She bakes a mean apple pie."

I tore a piece of crust off, nibbling as I joined him. "Agreed. Not bad."

"So, what's on your mind today, kid?" Derek asked, sipping at the steaming liquid.

I cleared my throat, not really sure where to start. If Aiden's news had stunned me last night, it was bound to freak out Derek. The last thing I wanted to do was give the guy a heart attack.

"I have some information regarding a past open case," I said, trying to ease into it.

"An *open* case?" he asked, his eyebrows furrowing together.

I understood his confusion. We didn't have many of those. Usually we stuck with a guy until we proved either he was cheating or his wife was paranoid. Very few remained "unsolved" in our particular line of work.

"Yes," I said. I looked down to his chest where I knew a large, circular wound was hidden under his stained T-shirt.

"I'll bite," Derek said. "Whose?"

"Yours."

He paused. "What do you mean, mine?" he asked, his voice flat, his eyes suddenly sharp, all sleep having been chased from them.

I cleared my throat again. "Aiden is trying the case of Jack Brady. You heard of him?"

Derek nodded. "He's the dirty cop, right?" he said, no indication of recognition beyond the media's version of the story registering on his face.

"Right. Well, while Aiden was prepping for the trial, it came out that the gun Brady used to shoot his victim was used in another crime." I paused. "Against you."

Derek's hand immediately went to his chest, an unconscious gesture I was sure. A range of emotions swam through his eyes, one after the other so rapidly I'd be hard-pressed to identify them. Finally they settled into something hard and unreadable.

"I see," he said, his voice tight. He grabbed his mug with both hands, sipping again.

"Look, I don't know what this means yet," I told him. "If Brady was the guy who shot you, or if he knows who did, or what. But I promise you, I'm going to find out."

But to my surprise, Derek shook his head. "No."

I blinked. That was the last thing I expected him to say. "No?"

"No. Leave it alone."

I cocked my head at him. "I'm sorry. I just give you critical information regarding a shooting—*your* shooting—that has been unsolved for three years, and you want me to just leave it alone?"

Derek looked up from his coffee, his eyes softer. "Look, James, where there's one dirty cop, there are more. You don't cover up things like murder on your own. Leave this to Aiden. I don't want you getting involved."

While his words said *I'm worried about you*, his eyes said something else. Something along the lines of, *I don't trust you to handle something this big*.

"Derek, Aiden is busy with the trial. Your shooting isn't his case. It's not even on his radar until there's an arrest."

"Did he hand the evidence over to the original investigators?" Derek asked.

I paused. Good question. One I hadn't specifically asked. "I-I would assume so," I told him.

Derek nodded. "Good. Then let them handle it. If there's a connection, they'll find it."

"But—" I started to protest.

But Elaine picked that moment to come out of the bedroom, clothed now in a pair of stretchy capris and a tank dress that was clinging to her body tighter than a boa constrictor. "Sorry to interrupt, but I gotta go. I'm late for work."

"It's okay," Derek said, standing. "James was on her way out, anyway."

I pursed my lips together. I hadn't been. But clearly this was Derek's way of saying he was done talking.

"Nice to see you again," I said to Elaine. Then to Derek, "We'll talk later."

He gave me a stiff nod.

I walked back up to the top deck, then got into my car. I watched as Elaine emerged a moment later, Derek attached to her hip, giving her a kiss with more tongue than I ever wanted to see. Then she stumbled over the gangplank, leopard printed pumps in hand, toward a Honda Civic parked a few slots down. Derek watched her go, then slipped back down into the *Black Pearl* without so much as glancing my way.

I chewed my lip. If I'd just found out someone might know who had tried to kill me, I'd be a lot more into finding out who than Derek was. Maybe reliving the incident was too much for him. Maybe telling me to leave it alone was his macho way of saying he couldn't deal with this. Though I had a hard time picturing Derek as vulnerable, his tough shell held a fragile ticker that, since the shooting, was on three different kinds of medications to keep it going. Maybe his heart really couldn't take this.

Maybe.

But one thing was for sure. My heart was fine, I could take reliving it, even the rough moments, and I did not have Derek's faith in the over-worked original investigator's interest in following up on a three-year-old cold case.

And there was no way I was leaving this alone.

# CHAPTER FOUR

———

I parked a few houses down from Jack Brady's Spanish-style stucco bungalow in Burbank. As I expected, the press were camped out on his sidewalk, waiting for a camera-worthy moment. A few were slumped against the curb roasting in the sun, while the others sat in their cars with their windows rolled up, undoubtedly blasting the A/C.

Brady's black SUV sat in the driveway, and going off of the three drive-bys I'd done before parking, it hadn't moved in the last forty-five minutes. With the trial starting in the morning, it was unlikely he would go out today.

I needed to talk to Brady, and Brady wasn't budging. Which meant I had to get into that bungalow. Luckily, I'd already run through several possible roles I could play to get through his front door, and I'd arrived prepared.

I flipped down my visor and surveyed myself in the attached mirror. My chestnut brown wig sat slightly crooked. I pulled on the pigtails, readjusting the center part before glancing down at the denim shorts and red blouse I'd grabbed from my apartment. I prayed I'd pass for a delivery person. The research I'd done on Brady gave me precious little information. Looking for leads online was as effective as starting my day without caffeine. But I had found one tagged Facebook photo of him with his girlfriend, a busty brunette. I prayed I passed for his type as I unbuttoned the last three buttons on my shirt and tied the fabric into a knot above my navel. I grabbed a box of Papa Gino's large supreme from my passenger seat and climbed out of my car.

As my heels click-clacked against the pavement, the news guys turned and smiled. At least I had someone's attention.

"Hello, boys." I smiled and kept up my don't-derail-me-I-gotta-get-naked-soon pace.

"That sure smells good," one of them bellowed. "Want to share?"

"Another time," I called, waving him off with my free hand.

I turned up the walkway and hurried along the cracked stone. While the news crews weren't camped out directly on Brady's front lawn, I felt them close in as I approached the door. I had no doubt they'd use my arrival as a way to capture any pictures of the accused that they could.

I grabbed the wrought iron knocker, struck it against the door twice, and waited. And waited. A car door slammed behind me, footsteps scurried. A quick glance over my shoulder told me the press still stood on the sidewalk, but they were poised for action.

I closed my fist and pounded on the door again, each whack matching each bead of sweat trickling down my back. "Delivery," I shouted.

The door flew open. "What is it?"

The guy's red face was contorted into a snarl. He wore a pair of jeans and nothing else, displaying a light smattering of golden hairs across his chest. He was older than I was by a good decade, a worn-hard look about him that said this current trial wasn't the first trouble he'd experienced in his life.

I flinched at his abrasiveness but kept my composure. Angry, naked men were a part of the job description.

"Delivery," I repeated, gesturing to the pizza in my hand.

His eyebrows drew together, gaze pinging from me to the vultures behind me.

I heard a camera go off and prepared to have the door slammed in my face. I stepped forward so I was just *this* much over the threshold. I donned a big, bright smile, and shifted the hot box to one hand, cradling it in the crook of my elbow. "You ordered a pizza?"

He blinked at the sunlight. The interior of the house was dim, and all I could make out were shadows of furniture. "No, I didn't."

"You sure?" I asked, leaning closer, doing my best giggling-flirt thing. "'Cause I could swear this had your name aaaaall over it," I said, drawing out the word in an obvious sexual innuendo.

Brady paused, his gaze slowly roving my body. The left side of his mouth curved up.

I smiled and wiggled my hips. "Hi, I'm Jamie."

Camera shutters clicked behind me again.

Brady briefly glanced over my shoulder. Then before I could react, he grabbed my arm and yanked me inside. I held onto the pizza box with both hands, hearing the eight slices slide back and forth. Good thing he hadn't ordered this because the cheese was probably sticking to the lid.

He slammed the door shut so hard my teeth chattered.

We stood in a small living room. The only source of light came from the flickering television in the corner. A blanket was crumpled on the sofa, and an empty plate sat beside a full ashtray and a bottle of Jack Daniels on the coffee table. No glass.

"Okay, Jamie, who sent you, and who are you really?"

Damn, he was good. Then again, he was a cop. And the dirty ones were even more suspicious than those who believed in upholding the law.

But I still played along, widening my eyes. "What do you mean?"

He smirked. "Ever since the robberies a few months ago, Papa Gino's only hires male drivers."

Well that's just sexist. And smart. And information I wish I'd had about half an hour ago

"So again, who are you, and what do you want?" His gaze shifted to my chest. Apparently, whoever I was, he didn't feel threatened by me. With his six-foot, daily-gym body, I couldn't exactly say the same.

"I was hoping we could talk."

"About?"

I figured I had nothing to lose by going the direct route. "The gun that you used to shoot Edward Bernstein."

His smile disappeared. "Get out."

"I just need a moment."

He braced the doorframe, brushing his torso against me. "I don't talk to the press."

I dug my heels into the threadbare carpet and shook my head. "I'm not a reporter."

He grabbed the pizza box from my hands and tossed it onto the coffee table, sending his plate to the floor. It spun then settled upright. He brought the liquor bottle to his lips and swallowed a shot's worth before facing me.

"You another lawyer? 'Cause in case you haven't heard, I have no use for them." His grin was bitter and menacing.

"I'm not a lawyer."

"Then you got two seconds to tell me who the hell you are before I throw your fine ass out on my porch."

I felt a chill between my shoulder blades, certain it wasn't an idle threat.

"I'm Jamie Bond," I responded, watching his reaction closely, then added, "Derek Bond is my father."

Brady's mouth tightened ever so slightly. "I got nothing to say to you."

Which told me the exact opposite. That little gesture was enough to say he was full of pertinent information.

"You know him?" I was becoming more and more convinced that Derek's shooting had nothing to do with the adulterous husband he'd been staking out, like everyone wanted me to believe, and everything to do with Brady.

But Brady didn't answer, instead growling, "Get out." He punctuated the command by reaching past me and opening the door with a jerk. Then he gripped my forearms and propelled me out the door as easily as if I were a rag doll.

"But I…"

And that's as far as I got before he stepped back and slammed the door in my face.

I stared at the closed door. "Nice talking to you, too," I shouted.

"Hey, what was that about, pizza girl?" one of the press asked as I walked back to my car. "Not enough cheese?"

Several of them laughed.

I resisted the urge to give them the finger as I headed back to my roadster. Once inside, I took a deep breath to slow my heart rate, then grabbed my cell from my purse, pulling up a screen with the notes I'd made earlier.

Okay, so Brady wasn't going to dole out information freely. No big surprise there. But that meant I needed to talk to someone who would. I flipped to the page with the name of Brady's girlfriend. She worked at a diner, the address a few blocks away. Hopefully she was a little more friendly.

* * *

According to her Facebook page, Jillian Granger waited tables at a retro, 50's style place that catered to tourists and studio types. Inside, black and white checkered floor tiles seemed to stretch for miles. The walls were covered in framed movie posters of stars from long ago: Grace Kelly, James Stewart, John Wayne, and of course Marilyn Monroe. An old-fashioned jukebox in the far corner played Elvis's "Hound Dog."

A waitress sporting an auburn beehive, white blouse, black poodle skirt and a red apron passed by carrying a tray of soft drinks. "Take a seat anywhere, hon, and we'll get to you."

Her name tag read: Brenda. She headed to a corner booth where four guys were bent over a script plastered with Post-it notes. The other side of the room held a lone man nibbling on a cheeseburger while reading *Variety*, a trio of men in their mid-forties wearing ties, and an older couple sipping on ice cream sodas.

The counter was empty except for the waitress behind it. She was loading straws into an old-fashioned dispenser. Her head was bent, focusing on her task, and she wore the same uniform as Brenda, except she was a brunette. And she didn't seem to have the bubbly vivaciousness of her co-worker. There was something solemn in her posture.

I approached the red Formica counter and sat on a matching vinyl stool.

Without glancing up, the woman asked, "What can I get you?"

I hadn't eaten in hours, and the scent of fries was almost unbearable. "Cheeseburger and fries. And coffee, please."

She nodded, writing up the ticket, then turning to a coffee pot and pouring a cup. When she placed it as well as a container of cream in front of me, she met my gaze and gave a weak smile.

Tiny lines circled her eyes. They were sad, like they'd seen too much heartache. Her name tag confirmed she was Brady's girlfriend.

"Food should be up soon," she said. "I wouldn't drink too much on an empty stomach." She nodded to my cup.

"Thanks." I stirred my usual amount of sugar and cream into my cup, but when the color hadn't lightened much, I realized she wasn't kidding. "Listen, Jillian, right?" I asked gesturing to her nametag.

She nodded again.

"I was wondering if I could talk to you for a minute."

She frowned at me. "Do I know you?"

I shook my head. "But your boyfriend knows my father."

Her jaw clenched. I couldn't tell if she and Brady were having couple issues (and who could blame them at a time like this) or if she too was going to demand I leave.

"I can't discuss the trial." She started to turn.

"This isn't about that. Please help me."

Maybe she felt sorry for me or maybe she identified with the desperation in my voice, because she faced me, cocking her head skeptically. "Help with what?"

I took a deep breath. "I'm simply looking for a connection between Jack and my dad, Derek Bond." I carefully watched her expression.

She didn't flinch or make the same indication Brady had that she recognized Derek's name. Which didn't really surprise me. Even though the info I'd dug up online said she and Jack had, indeed, been dating three years ago when Derek was shot, I hadn't assumed Brady told his girlfriend about his ill deeds.

"What kind of connection?" she asked, wrinkling her tiny nose, looking confused.

I didn't want to risk losing her help, so I spoke fast. "Anything. I already saw Brady, but he's not in the mood for company."

Her chest heaved, as if releasing a long held breath.

"Jillian, order," shouted a man's voice from the kitchen.

I glanced up and watched a stocky guy place three plates on the steel counter that separated the front and back of the restaurant.

"One sec," she whispered and loaded the plates onto a tray.

I sipped the diesel in my cup and grimaced. That was foul and should be illegal.

I watched Jillian approach the table with the three men and distribute the plates. One of them gestured to her breasts and made a joke I couldn't hear, but it sent his pals chuckling again.

Jillian frowned but didn't say a word. She just pulled a bottle of ketchup from her pocket, set it on the table, and walked off, her saddle shoes clicking along the checkerboard floor.

No wonder she looked…defeated. Working around pigs sucked.

When she returned, I said, "You don't have to put up with that."

She shrugged. "I do if I want to pay rent."

I opened my mouth to protest, but she stopped me by leaning her elbows on the counter and lowering her voice. "Look, I worked as an assistant to the CEO of a dot com company two years ago. They folded, and I was unemployed. In the thirteen months it took me to get hired here, I lost my home, had to move in with my never-getting-married boyfriend, and now I always smell like burgers. So if some jerk wants to talk about my tits, I'm not complaining as long as he tips well. And those guys are twenty percenters."

I felt myself smile and nodded my understanding. Who was I to judge? Not only had I experienced my share of touchy-feely guys as a model, but in a couple of hours I'd be dancing amongst those in their birthday suits at the "Bare Boogie".

"So why are you looking for a connection between Jack and your father?" she asked.

"It involves an old case. I'm a private investigator," I explained, keeping it purposely vague. "Jack may be able to help me clear some things up."

"And your father can't help 'clear things up?'" she asked, that skepticism creeping into her voice again.

"He, um…has a heart condition. The memories are a bit rusty." A half truth. "Plus he's a stubborn old goat." The full truth.

She smiled. "He sounds a lot like Jack."

"Do you know if they knew each other?" I asked her.

She shrugged. "I could ask Jack."

"Yeah? That would be great."

"But don't get your hopes up," she warned me. "Jack talks about what he wants to when he wants to. And usually that's not much with me lately." She frowned, her mind clearly going to the upcoming trial.

"When are you working next?" I asked.

"Morning shift Monday through Friday. Today was a double. I'll be here tomorrow morning." She grabbed a rag and began absently wiping down the counter.

She wasn't going to be at the trial and show her support to the jury? I must've looked surprised because she shrugged.

"He doesn't want me there. Says it's best if I don't get involved."

She grabbed a napkin and turned her back to me, her movements suggesting she was dabbing at tears.

What a turd. Not only was Brady a dirty cop, he was a heartbreaker, too.

Jillian took a moment to compose herself. Brenda grabbed my cheeseburger from the back, delivering it as I watched Jillian take off for the ladies' room.

Half a burger and a handful of very greasy fries later, she reemerged but averted her eyes from me. Whether she was hiding something or just ashamed at becoming emotional over a loser like Brady, I couldn't tell. But she didn't come back to the counter.

I finished my meal and put a twenty and my business card down next to my plate before leaving.

As I walked to the door, Mr. Tits-Jokes beckoned Jillian over again, and tips or no tips, I felt distinctly sorry for the woman.

# CHAPTER FIVE

———

Half an hour later, I was back at the office and running late to meet Caleigh and Sam. I quickly changed back into my cover-up that covered almost nothing up, and grabbed my purse just as Danny texted me that he was outside. I locked up the office and rode the elevator down to the ground floor, praying I didn't meet anyone else on my way out. Luckily, the building's lobby was empty, and I had a clean getaway to Danny's waiting surveillance van. I climbed into the passenger side and slammed the door shut. The second I was seated, my eyes immediately went to his attire. He wore a pair of black Speedos. And nothing else.

I swallowed hard.

"Wow."

While Danny had seen me nearly naked on several photo shoots when I was younger, I realized that I'd never seen him in anything but board shorts or jeans. I had to admit, the sight was not altogether unpleasant. I struggled to bring my eyes up to meet his.

Which were grinning with undisguised enjoyment.

"Was that a 'wow' I just got?"

I cleared my throat, feeling my eyes stray south again. "Maybe."

"Are you checking out my package, Bond?" Danny asked, the hint of a smile in his voice.

I forced my eyes up again, my cheeks going hot. "Just a little."

"Like what you see?" he teased.

I shrugged. "I've seen worse."

"Honey, you ain't seen nothing yet," he told me, the corners of his mouth crinkling upward in a grin that was positively wicked.

It was the "yet" that got me. I felt the heat in my cheeks traveling south toward the region of my lacey thong. I sniffed, trying to feign disinterest. And doing a crap job of it, I might add. "I'm surprised you aren't going all the way, Danny. I didn't peg you as shy."

Danny winked at me. "The night is young, babe."

Oh, boy.

I took a few deep breaths, telling myself that I had no interest whatsoever in Danny's innuendoes, as I let him man the radio. He fiddled with the dial as we merged onto the freeway, finally settling on an oldies station that was playing The Temptations.

I let my mind wander over Brady and Jillian as I watched billboards and graffiti laden overpasses whip past the window. I had to wonder what had attracted her to the guy in the first place. Was it the power? She go for the bad boy type? I wondered exactly how much she knew about what Brady had been into. From the news stories I'd read, he was being accused of everything from beating confessions out of suspects to taking bribes for favors. Which made me wonder what the hell he had to do with Derek. While Derek's moral compass was slightly off point, I'd never known him to actually harm anyone. Skirt the law at times in pursuit of a mark, yes. But not the caliber of stuff that Brady was accused of. So why would Brady shoot Derek? Or was there even a connection there beyond the gun?

"Earth to Jamie."

I started in my seat, turning to face Danny. "What?"

He frowned at me under his sandy brows. "Wow, you really have tuning me out down to a science, huh?"

I shot him a sheepish grin. "Sorry. A lot on my mind. What were you saying?"

"I was just asking how much farther this place is."

I glanced out the window to get my bearings. The billboards had given way to pine trees and jagged rocks. "A couple more miles. It's on the right."

Danny nodded. "So what's on that mind of yours?" he asked, eyes cutting sideways to me.

I shrugged him off. "Nothing. Stuff," I answered, realizing how lame that sounded as soon as it left my mouth.

"Uh-huh."

A Four Tops song popped on the radio, and I took the opportunity to change the subject. "Exactly how old are you?" I teased, gesturing to the radio.

Danny shook his head at me. "This is a classic, Bond. It's timeless."

"It's old."

"What do *you* want to listen to? Got a Beiber CD in your purse?" he shot back.

"The very fact that you used the term 'CD' just proved my point."

Danny shot me a look, then turned up the volume on his oldies fest.

I grinned, glad he'd dropped it. An interrogation was the last thing I wanted, especially considering what the rest of the night held.

Naked boogying.

I shuddered. Somehow I almost preferred the thoughts of murder trials, gun shots, and dirty cops. I had a bad feeling I was going to see things tonight that would scar my mind for life.

Fifteen minutes later we were knocking on the door to Sam and Caleigh's room.

"Everyone decent?" I called. "Danny's with me."

Caleigh cracked the door. "Is he in the buff?" she asked, peering over my shoulder.

I opened the door all the way and headed inside. "Not yet, but the night is young," I said, repeating his threat. I caught him grinning behind me as I flopped onto the scratchy, tweed sofa, clutching the hem of my cover-up, careful not to expose any of my girly parts. "How'd this afternoon go?" I asked.

Sam sat at the dinette and attached a hidden video camera decoyed as a round, shiny yellow smiley face pinned to her collar. It was bright and hideous, but cute at the same time. "Caleigh's been brushing up against Martin all day with no luck."

"I'll get him tonight though. I can feel it," Caleigh said, adding her choice of surveillance equipment around her neck—a gaudy red pendant on a gold chain. Inside the fake red stone sat a camera that took sixty high res photos per minute. The downside was that it only had four gigabytes of space, so she'd have to work him fast.

Danny handed me the last gadget on the table. A silver bobby pin with a large purple flower disguising the camera.

"For you, my dear," he said, brushing my hair behind my ear and pinning the camera there. It might have been my imagination, but I could have sworn his hand lingered a second longer than it needed to.

I cleared my throat. "Are we ready?" I asked, taking a conscious step away from Danny.

"Just a sec," Caleigh said, pulling out a tube of candy apple red lipstick.

I sat on the bed as I watched her apply it in the bathroom mirror, then add blush and an extra swipe of mascara. I jiggled my knee up and down with nervous anticipation.

Suddenly I felt a warm hand on it.

My eyes shot to my right. Danny was staring at my knee, his large hand holding it still.

"You okay, James?" he asked, his voice low.

I cleared my throat again. "Yeah. Fine. Why?"

He shrugged. "You just seem a little…off tonight."

"I'm fine," I said. "I'm just…not looking forward to the dance." Which was the truth even if it wasn't what had me on edge.

"Don't worry," he reassured me, that familiar teasing note creeping into his voice. "You're not *that* bad of a dancer."

I turned on him. "Hey, I'm a great dancer."

Danny pursed his lips. "Really? Define great?"

"I'll remind you of that club in Rio. We danced until daylight, and not once did I step on your feet. You, however, bruised my pinky toe."

He shook his head, his expression serious. "Nope. I refuse to believe that. It had to be the other way around."

I couldn't tell if he was joking or not. But before I could insist, Caleigh tossed her lipstick in a little handbag and turned to the room at large. "Let's do this," she said.

Danny jumped up and grabbed her arm. "Lead me to the naked ladies."

We headed out and walked down to the main building where silver and gold helium balloons were tied to the wrought-iron railings flanking the front doors. Inside more balloons and matching streamers decorated the lobby and followed us into a white-walled, gym style room, complete with hanging, twirling disco ball lights and a DJ area.

So far, we were the only people there.

We made our way to a table with a punch bowl, a raw veggie plate with dip and an assortment of chips.

"Does anyone else get the feeling we're in junior high?" Sam whispered.

Danny picked up a broccoli stalk. "This is not what you want a group of naked people digesting."

Voices traveled from the lobby. The first gathering of people arrived, and it wasn't long before we were surrounded by nakedness. All of them, including the DJ. I wasn't usually a prude, yet I couldn't shake the weirdness.

Caleigh sauntered over to Martin, who was speaking to a man with rich brown hair on his head and gray everywhere else. Martin acknowledged her with a smile and allowed her to press against his side, but he didn't stop talking to Mr. Two-Tone.

"This is...um, interesting." Danny scanned the crowd.

I followed his gaze to a couple of women talking by the door. They appeared to be in their early forties and mothers. I patted him on the shoulder. "Stretch marks can be sexy. And right about now, I'll say, I-told-you-so."

Danny smirked. "Hey, I'm not above a cougar or two."

I looked back to the moms. If I had to guess, I'd say the only cougars they knew were the mascots of their kids' soccer teams. "Yeah, good luck with that," I told him.

Music began, a fast beat full of bass. Several couples moved into the center of the dance floor. They swayed, gyrated, and got funky, all without a care that some of their parts were jiggling and flopping. I averted my eyes and tried hard not to laugh.

Caleigh was dancing with Martin on the far side of the room. I couldn't make out if he was just being friendly or being *friendly* friendly. Sam danced by herself over at the DJ's table. She had a straight line to Martin, but couples kept blocking her view. Which meant I needed to get closer.

I grabbed Danny's hand and pulled him into the crowd. "Come on."

"Why, yes, I'd love to dance with you, Bond," he shouted over the music.

I angled us diagonally from Martin. As long as he and Caleigh didn't moonwalk across the room, I had the perfect shot for adulterous foreplay.

I moved to the beat, keeping Caleigh in sight. As one song blended into another, I felt myself getting lost in my thoughts about Derek and Brady again and praying Jillian would come through and give me the missing piece to the puzzle tomorrow. Even though I knew it was a long shot. Why would Brady suddenly confide in his girlfriend now if he hadn't in all these years? But long was the only kind of shot I had at the moment.

"You're doing it again."

I blinked and the room refocused. "Huh?"

Danny narrowed his eyes at me. "Where were you?"

I shook my head to clear my thoughts, as if that could literally happen. "Thinking of a case."

"I thought *this* was your case."

I looked into his eyes. In the past, Danny would've been the first person I shared my troubles with, but this one felt too personal. Like it only existed for Derek and me, and no one else was allowed in on it.

"Yeah. This case. It doesn't look like Caleigh's making any headway."

He glanced over his shoulder. Caleigh and Martin were still dancing, still the same distance apart. "Give it time. She can work her magic."

The song ended and instead of another fast dance tune, a slow ballad came on. The kind you'd belt out while alone in your car, with the windows raised. Before I had a chance to step off to the side of the room, Danny grabbed my hands and pulled me closer.

Heat from his body seared through my thin cover-up, suddenly making me all too aware of how little we were wearing and how close together we were standing.

"What are you doing?" I asked.

Danny gave me a funny look. "It's called dancing, Bond. Why are you acting strange tonight?"

I wished I had an answer.

"We need to keep Martin in view," Danny added.

I glanced across the room. Martin was still on the floor, though I noticed he had Caleigh at an arm's length now.

Right. I swallowed, ignoring the pressure of Danny's torso against mine. We were manning the camera. That's it.

Danny held one of my hands level with his chest and slid his other arm around my waist, cupping the small of my back as he swayed me to the right, making sure my hairpiece was aimed at Martin. I closed my eyes and took a deep breath, telling myself not to inhale the scents of warm aftershave and strong soap wafting toward me.

"You were so young." His voice was husky, his breath ruffling the top of my hair.

I pulled back, looking him in the eye. "What are you talking about?"

"The dance in Rio."

"You do remember."

A smile tugged the corners of his mouth up. "Of course. It's one of my best memories of us."

The way he said the word "us" stirred something in my belly. Not the way my best friend would talk about a party we crashed together. More the way a lover would remember a stolen night in a faraway place.

I swallowed hard, my body tensing as I watched his eyes fall back onto the memory.

"You trembled in my arms. You tried to pass it off as the night breeze from the ocean, but I knew it was nerves."

"I was eighteen and terrified all the time," I said, brushing off the moment. Despite the glamour and constant attention, some great and some very critical, I hadn't a clue how to be a model or an adult back then. Mom was gone and Derek was… well, Derek. He didn't exactly have training in raising young ladies.

"You didn't show it," Danny said.

"That's why I was such a successful model. I knew how to fake it."

"You were a natural. Elegant, poised."

"I was a kid. I'm surprised you noticed."

He cocked his head at me. "You were eighteen. And I have a feeling, Bond, that you were never really a kid."

I looked away, trying to hide the truth of that from my eyes. "Yeah, well, that was a long time ago."

"It was. You're definitely not a kid anymore," he said, his voice low and filled with some meaning that I wasn't sure I wanted to try to interpret.

The song ended, and Danny let go of my hand, instantly putting distance between us, as if he didn't want to interpret that meaning any more than I did.

I tucked my hair behind my ear, glancing at Caleigh. The poor girl was still trying to slow dance closer to Martin. I mentally made a note to give her a raise.

I grabbed a cup of punch and positioned myself near the DJ to catch any misdeeds. Sam stood opposite from me, moving every now and then to find a better angle. Danny mingled, chatted with the "cougars," glanced every now and then at our mark. Caleigh danced her butt off, and chatted and giggled as if she was actually on a fun date. Every once in a while, she'd look my way and roll her eyes for the camera.

When the night finally ended, he still hadn't hit on her.

"You think he's ever going to bite?" Sam asked after we walked back to our room. She grabbed a bottle of water from the mini-fridge.

"Absolutely. He's warming up. I can tell." Caleigh sat on the sofa and slipped off her heels, looking like she was ready for a hot shower and long night's sleep.

"We'll give it until the end of tomorrow. If he doesn't try something by then, I'll give the report to his wife," I decided. Though I didn't share Caleigh's hopefulness. She was a stunning woman. If Martin hadn't taken the bait yet, what would change his mind in a day?

"I wish I could stay," Sam said. "But the babysitter can't spend the night."

Guilt wormed its way through my body. I would've loved to stay as well. A slumber party with liquor. But I couldn't relax until I had answers about Derek's shooting. I wouldn't be good company, and there was still more digging to do.

Caleigh waved a hand. "I don't mind. Really. I'm going to crash as soon as y'all leave."

"I'll be back first thing in the morning," Sam promised.

"And I'll be along by the afternoon," I added.

No one asked why, but they all stared.

"I gotta take care of something for Derek," I mumbled.

No one pressed further, though I could feel questions swirling in the air.

Join the club.

# CHAPTER SIX

———

Danny dropped Sam and me off at the agency parking lot, saying something about an early photo shoot in the morning before taking off. After he left, I gave Sam a wave and a,"'Night, Sam," then watched her walk to her car.

I grabbed the door handle on my roadster, pretending I was leaving too, and watched her pull out. It was foolish to hide my actions from Sam. I was a big girl. If I wanted to work late, I could. But I didn't want to lie about what I was doing either.

After a quick change back into my street clothes, I sat at my desk, turned on the light beside my computer, and pulled up my Google research on Brady. This felt foolish and unproductive. Googling was for researching Chicken Piccata recipes and reading the latest celebrity gossip. But I'd already run his financials and checked into everything personal. It all led nowhere. Derek hadn't appeared to be connected to any part of Brady's life. So this is what I was left with. If nothing panned, I'd have to get Maya or Caleigh involved. Their computer skills were a million cuts above mine.

I clicked the first link when I heard the agency's glass doors open and footsteps whoosh across the carpet.

What was Sam doing back here?

As I listened, my heart lodged in my throat. Those weren't female footsteps.

Damn, I'd been so preoccupied with Brady that I forgotten to lock myself in. I reached toward my gun, strapped to my holster, as the figure rounded the corner and stood in my doorway.

The light cast shadows on his face, but it lit up the legs of his Brooks Brothers slacks. Aiden.

My hand flew to my chest and my relief turned into an extended nervous chuckle.

He raised his brows and stepped inside. "I didn't mean to scare you."

"It's okay. I should've locked up. What are you doing here?" I glanced to my computer screen and stood, meeting him on the other side of my desk. There was no crime in googling someone, but I didn't want him jumping to the right conclusions.

"I was on my way home and saw your car."

His home—a condo off Wilshire. I drove by once, just wanting to catch a glimpse of where he rested after a hard day of work. Okay, and maybe to check up on him a little. What can I say? The investigator in me was hard to silence. Unfortunately it was a gated community, and I couldn't get in without being announced.

His eyes looked tired, his jacket crumpled.

"You have a big day tomorrow," I said, referencing Brady's trial.

He nodded. "Bright and early."

"Do you think you'll win?"

"I never lay odds on a case. And it's not about winning. It's about justice."

Times likes this, I knew Aiden was way too "good" for me. I think I was about ten when I stopped believing in the fairytale of any sort of real justice being served by the American courts system. We fell into a silence, each thinking about our own ideas of right and wrong. It lasted just long enough to be awkward.

"Well, I should get going," Aiden finally said.

"Did you want something?" I asked, wondering why he'd stopped by in the first place.

He smiled in that confident way that made me question just how bad it would be to fall for a "good" guy.

"I just wanted to see your face," he said.

I grinned back at him. "Be still my beating heart."

He laughed, a chuckle that spread across the room to me. "Are you heading out? I'll walk you to your car."

I glanced at my computer. It could wait until tomorrow. Besides, if Jillian got the information I needed, Google would be a waste of time. I turned off the machine and collected my things.

Outside the night held a light breeze, cool around the edges, and a welcomed respite from the heat. This was my favorite time of day.

Aiden walked me to my car, held the door open, and leaned inside after shutting it. He smelled of fabric softener. Did he do his own laundry or have it done? Did he hire a cleaning woman to pick up after him? There were so many things I still didn't know about him.

A five-o'clock shadow lined his jaw. I wanted to reach up and caress the stubble, but we hadn't taken this to the touchy-feely level yet. But why should that matter? Just because he was ever so professional?

I lifted my arm…

"Goodnight, Jamie," he said, waved at me, and turned to go.

\* \* \*

I arrived at Hal's diner around eight. I had tossed and turned for the second straight night in a row, and this morning I felt like someone had replaced my blood with sludge. I finished my Macchiato, allowed the caffeine to worm its way through my brain cells, then headed inside.

The place was slammed this morning. Every table was occupied, and four waitresses worked the floor. Jillian was behind the counter again. I caught her eye. She gave me a busy, pained expression that clearly said I'd have to wait.

The jukebox coupled with the dinging kitchen bell, orders being shouted, the chatter of the crowd, and the cook barking made my head spin.

I'd figured there'd be a breakfast mob, but I anticipated it ending around now. Didn't people work?

After a few minutes, a man at the counter stood and left.

I hurried to the empty seat as Jillian wiped the area down. She poured me a glass of water. She looked more frazzled than yesterday. "Sorry, it's so crazy. I'll be with you as soon as I can. Do you want anything?"

The bell above the front door chimed, and two young women stepped inside.

I didn't want to take a potential tip away from Jillian, so I turned to the menu tacked to the wall. It listed at least thirty options, and I felt rushed to make a decision, so I blurted out, "Um, the special, please."

She nodded, wrote it down, and shouted to the line cook, before hurrying to the woman at the end and refilling her toxic coffee.

Jillian remained hectic and scrambling for a good ten minutes, and I wondered if I should come back later. But I only had a couple of hours before I needed to get back to the camp and finalize the Martin case.

Several neighboring customers left, and new ones took their seats. My order arrived: a steaming plate of French toast smothered in butter and powdered sugar. Jillian set a glass dispenser of syrup in front of it before rushing off to another customer.

It looked amazing, and tasted even better.

After my third forkful, Jillian finally stopped in front of me and took a deep breath. "Sorry about that. I should've mentioned we don't calm down until nine-ish."

"No problem. This is fabulous." I pointed to my half-eaten food.

"Makes up for the coffee, doesn't it?"

The customer to my right handed her a generous tip then left.

She cleared off his plate and cup and began wiping down the counter. "I talked to Jack last night."

I set down my fork, ready to hear all the juicy tidbits.

She shook her head. "He said he doesn't know any Derek Bond."

My shoulders slumped. "Are you sure?"

Jillian bit her lip. "I'm sure he said that, yeah." She paused. "But I think he's lying."

I leaned forward. "You do?"

She nodded. "I couldn't say why, but I just got the feeling he was holding something back."

In my experience, the girlfriend's lie detector was usually on point. "He wouldn't say what?"

She shook her head. "I pressed him, but he still denied it. I'm sorry I couldn't be more help."

I was too. But at least it confirmed what I'd already suspected from my own encounter with Brady. The name Derek Bond definitely meant something to him. I just had to find out what.

* * *

Before heading up to check on Caleigh and Martin, I went to the office and back to my unfinished googling. I instructed Maya I was not to be disturbed, then sat at my desk and typed in the keywords: Jack Brady Derek Bond.

The first page of links led to Brady's murder trial and his attorney, who happened to be named Derek Richmond. According to the reporter, Richmond was a shark in the courtroom. He rarely lost a case and wasn't above using tricks and games to get the jurors' sympathies.

Aiden would hate Richmond's tactics.

I clicked to the second page and scrolled through more articles that had nothing to do with Derek. Brady saving a small child from a car after it careened over an embankment. Brady accused of assaulting a suspect while taking him into custody. Brady named Police Officer of the Year by the city. Brady rumored to take bribes from members of a known drug cartel.

This case was far from black-and-white. Half the city believed Brady descended from the angels, while the other wanted his head on a platter.

At the bottom of the third page I spotted a link with the words Jack, Brady, and McNeil's in bold. The name sounded familiar. It led to an article about a domestic dispute between a drunken couple at McNeil's Bar three and a half years ago. Their verbal sparring escalated when the wife threw a glass at her husband's head, nicking him above the ear.

When the angered, and rightfully so, man grabbed his wife by the throat, Brady and his drinking buddy broke it up, quickly and effortlessly. The couple left, separately, and no charges were pressed. Whoever wrote the article made Brady and his associate sound like heroes.

A grainy photo showed the profile of Brady and the back of another man seated at the bar. As I ran my cursor over the picture, the arrow turned into a hand. I tapped on the touchpad and the photograph enlarged.

Both Brady and his friend wore jeans, work boots, and plaid shirts. This was a casual night out interrupted by the couple. So who was Brady's friend? If I could identify him, maybe he knew Derek.

I leaned closer and squinted. Two beers sat on the bar. The friend gripped his mug, as if he'd just set it down or was about to pick it up. His sleeves were rolled up a quarter of the way, and tattooed on his forearm was a…hook with a fish?

I gasped and sat up straight.

No, that was a mermaid wrapped around an anchor. I knew every line of that damn thing. I'd spent my childhood staring at it while on stakeouts.

It belonged to Derek.

# CHAPTER SEVEN

———

I leaned against the paneled wall and waited for Derek to emerge from his bathroom. I tried to ignore the swaying vessel and the queasiness in the pit of my stomach—not sure if was due to my diner breakfast or my current task. Derek had lied to me. Derek was hiding something.

Derek was about to get an earful.

The door opened and Derek flinched, his eyes widened, and he placed a hand over his chest. "Jesus, James, you scared the crap out of me."

I would have laughed at the bad pun, but I wasn't feeling that charitable toward him at the moment. "Hi, Derek."

He chuckled, shaking his head as he led the way into the galley. He grabbed a mug and poured thick, black coffee into it.

"Want some?" he asked, not turning around to meet my eyes.

"No, thank you."

Derek took his cup to the table. I followed, sliding into the seat across from him.

He held the cup to his mouth and took a long sip, staring at me the entire time. His eyes were full of questions. He knew something was up. How could it not be? I used to avoid spending time with dear old dad, and now here I was, at his doorstep twice in one week.

He set the mug down and swallowed hard. "Are you going to say something?"

Yes. I just wasn't sure how to broach the subject. I thought about each word, carefully played them out in my head on the ride over. I couldn't let him shoot me down again.

"You and Brady were drinking buddies," I blurted out. Nothing like the direct approach.

I watched his face, waiting for a mouth twitch, eyebrow raise, anything that would give him away. Before I saw a tell, though, he got up and poured more diesel into his cup. Classic avoidance move.

"You know Brady," I pressed.

He shrugged, back still to me. "I don't know what you mean."

I rolled my eyes. He was going to make me earn this confession. I opened my purse and pulled out a sheet of paper. The photo was even grainier after a trip through the office's cheap ink jet, but the tattoo was still visible enough that pressed up against Derek's arm it would be unmistakable.

"Busted." I pushed the paper across the table.

He took his time sipping before facing me again. He squinted, pretending he couldn't see it from his distance, but according to his last exam, his vision was 20/20. He stepped closer, the whole time probably churning a thousand excuses in his mind.

What was so secretive that he had to lie?

"Instead of finding a way out of admitting it, why don't you just come clean?"

I expected his brow to furrow, for color to rise into his neck, but that didn't happen. Instead, he continued his blind routine.

"That's your arm." I pointed to the tat. "You were drinking at McNeil's with Brady. Why didn't you mention that earlier when I brought up his name?"

One shoulder rose and fell. He sat across from me again, setting his mug on the photo, directly on the mermaid. No doubt on purpose. "It was just a drink."

"But you knew him."

"A drink," he said again, more forcefully this time. "It wasn't a big deal."

I scoffed. "Are you serious? The gun…his gun…"

Derek held up a hand. "I simply ran into Brady that night. I'd hardly call us buddies."

A chill settled across my shoulders as I watched his eyes avoid mine. "Then why didn't you just say that earlier?"

"It didn't seem relevant."

Bullshit. How dumb did he think I was?

I looked away, out to sea and the sunny horizon, anywhere but in his dark eyes. Was he somehow involved with dirty cops? How deep? Did he take bribes? Look the other way at illegal activity? It couldn't be true. Derek was fond of sin in magnitude from fast cars, fast women, and fast money, but I'd never known him to do anything criminal. Would I, though? Surely that wasn't something he'd flaunt to his daughter.

I faced him again.

He sipped his coffee, trying way too hard to be nonchalant.

"Did you know the guy Brady shot, too? Edward Bernstein? It happened right before you were shot."

He narrowed his eyes. "Is that supposed to mean something?"

"You tell me."

We stared at one another, and I would've given anything to know his thoughts right then.

He glanced away. "There's nothing to tell."

I shook my head. I didn't have time for this. I had naked old people to attend to. "I wasted hours finding out what you already knew, and now you can't even tell me the truth."

Now his brows furrowed and color rose into his cheeks. "No one asked you to. In fact, I explicitly told you to leave it alone."

"Excuse me for wanting to know who almost killed my father."

"It's not your case, James."

"It's my life!"

The words flew out of our mouths, both talking at the same time. I barely heard what he said, and I was certain it was the same for him. We were both too stubborn to surrender, and listening meant defeat, in some bizarre way.

"There's nothing to tell, so don't waste any more of your *precious* time," he spat out. Then he rose and walked to the back of the boat. His mug still sat on the photo, like some line drawn in the sand.

I resisted the urge to run after him, shake him, make him talk to me. Because we were clearly just talking in circles. He wasn't going to give me answers. If I wanted to know what happened that day, I'd just have to find out for myself.

* * *

When I arrived back at the agency to change into my nudist gear, Maya handed me a stack of messages. I shuffled through them. Most could be put off until later. One was from Aiden. I bit my lip. I'd meant to call and wish him luck with the trial this morning, but in all the Derek drama I'd forgotten. Maybe I could squeeze in a few minutes to stop by the courthouse before the session ended today and watch him in action. Only I had a few matters to attend to first.

I glanced up from my messages at the file cabinets that lined the wall behind Maya's desk. If I was going to get to the truth about Derek's shooting, I needed to dig deeper than Google.

Maya looked up from her keyboard and caught me staring. "Something wrong, boss?"

"When we first settled in here, what happened to Derek's old files?"

"They're in there," she said gesturing behind her. "With the others."

That's what I thought. I'd already gone through everything in those cabinets when I'd taken over the business. Derek might be a slob on his boat, but his files were meticulous. "How about anything else that Derek left behind?"

Maya scrunched up her nose in thought. Then she swung around and pointed to the far wall. "I moved some boxes into the storage closet. They were full of odd things like a broken pencil sharpener, some Christmas decorations, a little hula girl. You know, the kind people stick to their dashboards."

That sounded like Derek.

"There may have been some loose papers, too." Her expression was pained. "Sorry if I missed something."

"No, it's fine. Just curious."

"Do you want me to dig the stuff out?" She started to rise.

I held up my hand. "No. It's not important. I'll just have a look later."

She eyed me suspiciously for a moment, but then the phone rang and she returned to her chair.

I hurried to my office and slipped back into my cover-up. Ten minutes later, I was feeling far less covered, though much cooler. As if on cue, I heard the glass doors open in the lobby, then Danny appeared in my doorway, wearing the same pair of Speedos from last night.

"Oh, no," I said. "You can't seriously want to go back there?"

"Thought you could use the help," he said, shrugging, a carefree grin on his face.

"Didn't you have a photo shoot at the pier today?"

"Yeah, done."

"This early?" I asked, grabbing my purse.

"She was hung over from too many Jell-O shots last night. She yakked in the water."

"Eww, remind me not to swim there." Not that I had time to even think about heading to the beach.

"The director was pissed and told her to go home. I don't think he'll be hiring her again."

Modeling definitely had its perks, but I didn't miss the grueling hours under the sun or standing in freezing water and pretending it was warm and inviting.

"Since I'm free, I thought I'd give you ladies a hand."

"So, what, you didn't get enough cougar action last night? Hot girls aren't going to mysteriously appear this afternoon."

He pressed a palm against his chest in mock hurt. "Why do you assume I'm only about the women? Why can't this be about helping a friend with her case?"

I gave him a get-real look and shot back, "Says he of many bedded models."

Danny grinned and threw an arm around my shoulders. "That was a long time ago. You know I've only got eyes for you now, Jamie." He winked, and I couldn't tell if he was totally pulling my leg or there was some truth to the statement. Either way, I shrugged his arm off.

"Why do I find that hard to believe?" I mumbled.

"I don't know. Why do you?"

I placed a hand on my hip and stared him down. "Okay, Casanova, what did you do last night after dropping us off?"

The corner of his mouth quirked up. "Don't you mean who?"

I shook my head. "I rest my case."

Danny burst out laughing. "Jesus, James, I was kidding. I spent last night with a six-pack of beer and a marathon of *Storage Wars*. Come on, what kind of guy do you think I am?"

I paused, honestly a little surprised by the admission. "Quiet evening in" and "Danny" were two things that hadn't ever gone together in my mind before. Maybe I was wrongly judging him.

"Fine," I acquiesced. "You can come to the resort with me. But you're driving."

An hour and a half and three freeways later, we found Caleigh at the pool, lounging by Martin, and Sam at the bar sipping a Bloody Mary.

"Alcohol for lunch?" I asked, taking the stool next to her.

"It's a virgin. Unfortunately."

I glanced at our couple. Their chairs were side-by-side and Caleigh was on hers, practically slipping off and pouring herself onto him. Martin seemed almost uninterested.

"That boring, huh?"

"I'm starting to think this was a waste of time," Sam said.

I completely agreed but ordered a glass of orange juice anyway. Danny had wandered off as soon as we'd arrived. He probably found the one woman who sagged the least. I looked around but couldn't spot him.

Sam must've noticed my search because a grin sprang onto her face. "So you and Danny seemed rather cozy on the dance floor last night."

I waved a hand as if to say it was no big deal. Because it wasn't. "Just reminiscing about the past." Which was truthful enough.

"Sure." She nodded, sipping her drink, turning away and avoiding my eyes.

"What was that?"

"What?" She blinked up at me, all innocence.

"That look you just covered up."

"Nothing."

"Look, there is nothing between me and Danny," I told her. "There never has been."

"Right. Of course not."

"Our relationship is purely professional. It's a friendship. It's…"

Sam did some more blinking, her expression expectant, waiting for me to finish that thought.

"It's nothing," I finally finished.

"Hey, I never said it was anything. All I said was you looked happy dancing together."

I sipped my orange juice. "This needs alcohol," I decided.

Sam grinned. "I could swipe something from the mini-bar."

She had no idea how tempting that sounded. I took a few deep breaths, inhaling the rare fresh air, scented with a mix of pine trees and chlorine. I watched the bartender pour mimosas and more Bloody Mary's for the guests, his brown bangs falling over his blue eyes, adding a touch of charm to his all-American, pre-Scientology Tom Cruise look. I allowed the morning's dead ends to slip away. And I watched Caleigh do her thing, playfully, suggestively, and even lewdly touching Martin's arm and laughing at his jokes. He smiled and chatted. He even peered at her cleavage. But there was no butt squeezing, no exchanging of room keys. Not even a suggestive leer.

"I should've brought a book," Sam whispered.

Unfortunately, I didn't feel like laughing. It was time to call an end to this charade. Martin was obviously more interested in getting a lineless tan than hooking up.

I leaned toward Sam to say as much when an older gentleman, probably in his sixties, approached Caleigh. He leaned in and said something to her that caused her expression to go from playful to shocked to positively ill, all in the span of thirty seconds. What was that about?

She nodded, and as the older guy walked toward Sam and me, Caleigh bit her lip and shrugged our direction.

Oh, this wasn't going to be good.

Despite the deep wrinkles around his eyes and a bad case of sun spots on both his hands, he appeared in pretty good shape. Nothing hung that wasn't supposed to.

"Madams," he said with a tight grin.

"Hello, I am Samantha and this is Jamie." Sam held out her hand.

He shook it then moistened his lips with a dart of his tongue. I was pretty certain that was more action than Caleigh had seen in the past two days.

"Pleased to meet you both. I am Jon-Michael. I run this resort."

Sam and I exchanged glances. Even management felt the need to work in the buff. I briefly wondered what their mission statement looked like.

"Can we help you?" I asked, wondering if there was paperwork we forgot to complete.

His smile relaxed and broadened. "Yes. I've already spoken with your friends."

Plural? That must've included Danny too.

"As you can see, we offer a comfortable and secure environment."

"Yes," Sam said.

The orange juice began to sour in my stomach. I didn't like the placating tone in his voice.

"Well…" He fidgeted with his hands, rubbing the knuckles on his left hand to the point of distraction.

"Is there a problem?" I asked, praying he'd spit it out and move on.

He took a deep breath and slowly exhaled. "It's been brought to my attention that you lovely ladies are not enjoying our environment to the fullest."

Sam and I frowned at one another. She held up her drink. "We are. Wonderful cocktails."

He wrinkled his face, glanced at our chests, and shook his head. "No, dears, I mean the atmosphere. The reason we exist. I'm afraid if you aren't fully a part of the program, so to speak, then there is no reason for you to stay. We can refund any unused portion of your time spent…"

I held up a hand to cut him off. "What part of the program are we not complying with?"

His eyes widened. He waved a hand along the crowd. "Isn't it obvious?"

Okay, so maybe I was a bit naive, or maybe I simply wanted to act dumb so I wouldn't be forced to do what I assumed he was hemming and hawing about.

"Your clothes. They're making the other guests feel a bit uneasy. I'm afraid if you want to stay, you'll need to go au naturel like the rest of us."

Damn, he said it.

* * *

If I was a cartoon, my jaw would have been on the floor. I was under the impression that the place was clothing *optional*, not clothing *forbidden*. And I was about to tell Jon-Michael just that when Sam gripped the opening to her cover-up, ready to yank it off. She paused, clenched her teeth in a snippy grin. "Could you pretend you aren't staring?"

Jon-Michael turned six shades of red, from pink to plum, and scurried off, muttering his apologies.

"What are you doing?" I practically hissed the words.

She already untied the belt. "My job."

"But if Caleigh's not getting anywhere, and this is a waste, then let's just leave."

But as soon as the words tumbled from my mouth, everything changed.

At some moment during my shock, Caleigh had stood and disrobed. Not only had everyone, including the women, drawn in a breath, but she suddenly had Martin's undivided attention.

Of course.

Sam allowed her garment to slide off her shoulders and drape over the stool legs. She eyed my statue-like stillness. "Since when are you such a prude?"

I scoffed. I wasn't. But the sun was strong and I didn't want to burn. It wasn't like years ago. Now with the ozone layer and ultra-violet rays, one had to take extra precautions. Plus, I attached the pin camera to my cover-up. How could I capture footage if it was huddled into a ball on top of the bar?

I took a deep breath.

While those were all excellent excuses, even if I did say so myself, I realized it was time to man-up. Okay, so maybe I felt a bit uncomfortable disrobing in front of everyone. Was that so wrong? I'd posed half naked in front of cameras most of my life, but the truth was I was not fifteen anymore.

I glanced around, expecting to find all eyes on me, waiting for me to shed the material. My own striptease. I half-expected the jazzy tune on the speakers to switch to something slow and exotic. But no one was even paying us attention anymore. They were chatting and sunbathing. In fact, other than Caleigh's reveal, they ignored the three of us.

I did another deep breath, then I eased the fabric off, trying not to look too conspicuous, even though I heard Christina Aguilera singing Burlesque music in my head. I raised my glass to my mouth. The sweet, sticky juice brushed against my lips. I set it down and pushed it toward Tommy Jr. "Add some champagne, please."

Sam grinned but didn't turn my way. She kept her barrette camera aimed at our couple.

Caleigh and Martin stood on the far end of the patio, still within our shot, but not directly in the middle of the crowd. They leaned into one another, spoke in what appeared to be quiet tones. She smiled; he brushed hair from her shoulder. He said something, she chuckled, and he stared at the way her chest heaved. Then she leaned forward, he grabbed her ass, and our case was solved.

"Got him." I jumped off my seat, forgetting about my birthday suit for a moment, and instinctively draped one arm across my chest and my other hand below.

Ohmigod. I *was* a prude.

"That doesn't make you stand out." Sam nodded toward my hands.

Warmth crept into my neck and face. I let my arms hang naturally and edged back to my seat.

"We need more," Sam said. "Martin can talk away one butt-squish. We need him propositioning her."

Cheating husbands were notorious for weaving charming webs of lies, so I knew she had a point. I eased into a more nonchalant position. At least I hoped it appeared that way. But I was pretty certain I looked as strained as I felt. I turned my focus to Caleigh. And my drink. I ordered another. Who cared if I showed up to court tipsy?

Caleigh and Martin continued their dance. Two steps forward, one back, and a hand on her hip. Was he suddenly pretending to be coy? Why bother? She obviously hadn't minded his hand on her ass the first time. Another ten minutes of the same routine and my patience waned. I wasn't sure if my fidgeting had to do with my nakedness or desire to get to court before Aiden's first day went by without a showing from me, but each second seemed to crawl by at an agonizing pace. I wanted to run to the car, to break the speed limit and get back to civilization.

"Hey, you can handle this, right?" I asked Sam.

She glanced at me from the corner of her eyes. "Sure. In a rush?"

"I wanted to stop by the courthouse."

She smiled. "Checking in on the ADA, huh?"

"Something like that." I dug into my purse for my wallet. "We have it under control."

"Thanks. See you back at the office." I threw cash on the bar for our drinks. I needed to find my ride. Where had Danny wandered off to?

I slid off the stool, clutching my bag and cover-up, which I had every intention of putting back on. Jon-Michael would have to get over it. It was only a matter of minutes before we no longer needed to stay here anyway. I was struggling with the fabric in the sticky heat, when I finally spotted Danny on the far side of the clubhouse.

I froze.

As Jon-Michael had requested, Danny had ditched the Speedos. And I couldn't help letting my gaze stray downward. My cheeks heated to a bright red that had nothing to do with sunburn as I got a look at just why Danny's dates always left his apartment wearing big goofy grins.

Oh, *boy*.

# CHAPTER EIGHT

———

Unable to face Danny with a straight face, I slipped back to the bar and begged to borrow Sam's car. She handed over the keys, and I left her and Caleigh to wrap up the Martin case with a pretty little bow. I pressed the speed limit as I raced back to the office, changed, then made my way to the courthouse. When I slipped into a seat in the back, Aiden was standing up front with his back to me. His co-counsel, a dark-haired woman in an expensive looking suit, sat at the prosecution's table, furiously scribbling notes onto a legal pad. I was pretty sure she'd prefer a tablet, but those sort of electronics were forbidden in the courtroom. Too easy for part of the proceedings to suddenly end up on YouTube.

Aiden faced the witness box. A young, pinched-faced guy who looked distinctly uncomfortable in his cheap suit sat under his scrutiny. He was wearing a badge that identified him as one of LAPD's finest, and the guy's skin was pink and a thick sheen of sweat rested on his forehead, noticeable all the way at the back of the room. Nerves?

This room didn't have windows. I'd never been in it before, yet it still made my pulse race after my near-miss trial a few months ago when I'd first met Aiden. It was so much nicer sitting as a spectator than the accused, wrongly or otherwise.

"Officer Wylie, you were the first to arrive to the nine-one-one call about sounds of gunfire at 346 Los Padres Drive, correct?"

"Yes."

"Who lives at that address?"

He cleared his throat. "Jack Brady."

"When you arrived, what did you find?"

Wylie's eyes shifted to Brady, the twelve jurors, and back to Aiden, quick movements like a snake's tongue. Was he scared of Brady or the blue line? Cops didn't rat on other cops. They lived by a code, and while Aiden was one of the good guys, they were still on the other side of that line.

"The residence was dark, and Brady's car was in the driveway. The front door was ajar, so we went inside."

"We?"

"My-my partner, Officer Dunne, and I." Wylie pulled at the knot in his tie.

"Go on, please." Aiden stepped to his left, blocking the officer's view from the defense table. Smart move if Wylie's darting behavior was nerves. Without staring at Brady, or being stared at, perhaps the guy could concentrate on his testimony.

It seemed to work. Wylie's shoulders noticeably relaxed. "We walked through each room. Nothing looked wrong until we reached the back bedroom. A lamp was on the floor; its table knocked over. There were obvious signs of a struggle."

"Anything else?"

"A man was on the rug, bleeding from a gunshot wound to the chest."

Brady shot the guy in his own bedroom? What the hell happened that night?

Wylie continued, "Jack Brady sat on the edge of the bed."

"And the man on the floor?"

"I checked for a pulse, but he was already dead."

"And did you later ascertain that the deceased was Edward Bernstein, a criminal attorney?"

"Yes."

"Okay, so you walked into the room, saw the man on the floor…and what was going on with the defendant?"

The defense attorney, Richmond, stood. "I object. The witness cannot know my client's mental state."

Before Judge Noone, a middle-aged woman oddly reminiscent of Judge Judy, could reply, Aiden said, "I just want the witness to state what he saw. Was the accused crying in a corner or jumping for joy?"

I smiled. Aiden did have a way with words.

"Your honor," Richmond shouted.

Judge Noone raised a hand, palm out, to silence everyone. "Strike the counselor's last statement from the record. The jury is to disregard the prosecution's posturing."

"Thank you, your honor." Richmond returned to his seat.

The judge pointed to him. "But your objection is overruled."

Even from the back of his head, I could see the small smirk that lined Aiden's mouth. "Officer Wylie, please describe what you saw in regards to the defendant."

Wylie ran a hand through his short hair, making the spiky ends stand more erect. "Um, Brady was just sitting there, shoulders slumped."

"Was he holding a weapon?"

Wylie nodded. "Yes. A 9mm."

"Was it his service pistol?"

Wylie wiped his forehead with the back of his hand. "No."

"Did he say anything?"

"That Mr. Bernstein had broken in and tried to shoot him."

Aiden turned ninety degrees and faced the jury. "Did the deceased have a weapon on him?"

"No."

"Were any guns registered under Mr. Bernstein's name?"

"No."

"So as far as we know, Mr. Bernstein never owned a gun and didn't bring one to Brady's residence?"

"Yes."

Aiden just stood there for a heartbeat, giving the jury a few seconds to digest this information. I hadn't known he possessed a dramatic flair. It looked good on him.

"I have no further questions." Then he turned to walk back to his seat. As he did, his eyes roved the room, locking briefly on mine.

I smiled and did a little one-finger wave in his direction.

A slight nod of his head was all I got in return before he sat, facing the judge again.

I tamped down a flutter of disappointment. I mean, what

did I expect? It's not like he could blow me kisses from across the courtroom.

"Your witness, Mr. Richmond," the judge said.

Richmond was already on his feet. "Officer Wylie, were any other guns found in Mr. Brady's home?"

Wylie opened his mouth and frowned, perhaps unsure how to answer. "You mean…"

"Any weapons at all?"

"Yes. We recovered a second gun in the bedside table."

"And was this gun registered to anyone?"

"Yes, Jack Brady."

Richmond tapped his temple with his fingers. That was either his normal way of processing his thoughts, or he was now the one posturing for the jury. "And the gun that my client was holding when you found him, who was that registered to?"

"Um…no one."

I watched Richmond's profile. He gasped in mock surprise. "How can that be?"

This must've been what the article meant by Richmond's courtroom antics. His routine reminded me of Joe Pesci in *My Cousin Vinny*, except Brady wasn't some innocent kid like Ralph Macchio's character. Brady was one of the bad guys. And this wasn't fiction.

"It's what's considered to be a street weapon. The serial number had been filed off, so any previous owners can't be traced." Wylie grinned, wide, to the jury, as if proud to be schooling us common folk on big police terms. He probably spent his days off watching reruns of *Law & Order*.

"Is it possible…" Richmond paused, pointing toward Aiden. "I know you're not an expert, Officer Wylie, but is it *possible* that Mr. Bernstein brought the murder weapon to Mr. Brady's house, and, during a struggle, my client took the gun from his assailant and shot him in self-defense?"

Aiden jumped up. "Your honor…"

I tuned out his objection, laden with legalese, and focused on the jury. A couple of young women giggled at Richmond's theatrics. He was a striking man, dark hair, light eyes, a tall and fit physique, if you were attracted to sewer rats. So Brady claimed it was self-defense and not his gun. Was he lying? And if he wasn't, then the gun that shot Derek belonged to Bernstein. Had Bernstein had a beef with Derek? I added him to my mental list of people to check up on.

The judge banged her gavel, pulling me from my thoughts. "Overruled."

Aiden sat down and glanced back at me, almost apologetically. I knew it pained him to lose a jury point to Richmond. Twice as much for me to witness it.

Richmond repeated his long-winded question to Wylie again.

Wylie shrugged. "I guess." From the scrunched up look on his face, he obviously hadn't thought it possible on his own. He thought Brady was guilty, too.

I glanced at my watch. I needed to get in touch with the girls and arrange to meet with Mrs. Martin, but I didn't want to leave yet. I hoped I'd witness Aiden score a home run first.

"No further questions." Richmond turned on his heel and returned to his seat. A smug look stretched across his face.

"You may step down, Officer Wylie," the judge said.

In that instant, Brady turned in his seat to survey the courtroom, and he spotted me. Confusion swam across his expression, probably him trying to picture me with brunette pigtails. I hadn't been afraid of him when I approached him at his house, but something in the eyes now made my stomach squirm.

Without taking his gaze off me, Brady leaned to Richmond and whispered in his lawyer's ear.

"Mr. Prince, call your next witness."

"I call Fred Dwyer to the stand."

I couldn't take my eyes off Brady. Aiden's warm voice washed over me, trying to thaw the chill running through me. Brady's eyes were hard. Calculating. This was a guy no one would deny was dangerous.

Richmond turned and stared at me, whispering something in return to his client.

I blinked and looked ahead, trying to pretend I was just an observer here.

Aiden glanced at Brady and must've followed his glare, because Aiden turned to me. Brows furrowed, he shrugged as if to ask, "What's going on?"

I shook my head and slung the strap of my purse onto my shoulder. This definitely wasn't the place to get into it, and I wasn't quite ready to admit I'd visited Brady. In hindsight, knowing what I just learned about the night Bernstein died, it had been a brash decision to go alone.

The doors swung open and Fred Dwyer, a pencil thin man with a bad toupee, walked in. When he passed my aisle, I stood and hurried out. I'd deal with Aiden's questions later.

* * *

I opened the box marked DB in black Sharpie and sat on the office floor. There had been three boxes stuffed into the corner, beneath the Valentine decorations (which Maya and Caleigh insisted on hanging every year) and other holiday paraphernalia. The others boxes had held miscellaneous items just like Maya had said—the Hula dancer, a pair of fuzzy dice (really, Derek?), and other oddities. This last one didn't rattle like the others, but I wasn't holding my breath for secret diaries.

Dust puffed up and I sneezed. Twice. Rummaging through old boxes was exactly how I loved to spend my nights. It was up there with laundry and washing windows. Two tasks I didn't do often enough. Filtering through the box, I uncovered receipts, stacks of the short, white slips of paper held together in little packs by rubber bands. I grabbed the nearest stack and untied it, shuffling through. They showed a pattern in Derek's habits. Coffee and three donuts at two a.m. A meatball sub at three in the afternoon. Pork rinds and a Red Bull. It was a wonder his heart hadn't given out sooner.

Beneath several layers of stacks was a leather bound book. I pulled it out and stared at the gold initials monogrammed in the bottom right corner. DBM. Derek Matthew Bond. Maybe I'd hit the jackpot after all.

I opened and stared at a ledger. At first glance, it appeared to be the books for the agency. Derek hadn't been convinced computers weren't evil, a way for Big Brother to spy on your business. I tried to explain they were necessary in today's world, but he hadn't wanted to hear it. That was four years ago. Today, his militant views on computers had weakened, but he still believed the Internet did more harm than good.

But the more I looked at the ledger, the less I was convinced it was a simple accounting system. There were no totals anywhere. I realized it wasn't financial records but some kind of file system. Dates, initials, four digit numbers. I flipped to the date Derek had been shot. April tenth, three years ago. There was no entry for that date, but there was one two days earlier. And it was easy to find because it was the last entry. After that Derek had been in the hospital, and his files had been packed up by a moving company I'd tearfully hired to clean out his office. I stared down at the last entry.

0408/RBS/0178

What the hell did it mean? The date before that was 0330/ABM/0177. Assuming it stood for date then client's initials, what did the last number stand for? I could call Derek and ask, but I wasn't certain he'd be honest. And I'd rather not have him know I was still digging. It saved me from having to buy stock in Advil.

There was nothing else in this box. I pushed it back into its original spot, turned off the overheard bulb, and shut the door, taking the ledger with me. The lobby was dark except for a tiny glow from the printer Maya forgot to turn off and a shadowy light from an outside street lamp. I'd parked in a far, dark corner of the parking lot and locked the agency door behind me when I came in. No interruptions. Not that I wouldn't have welcomed Aiden's company, but I wasn't ready to share what I'd learned. Aiden was a black and white kind of guy when it came to the law. I wasn't sure how he'd feel about Derek and Brady being old drinking buddies.

At least not until I knew that was all they'd been.

I sat in Maya's chair and stared at the room from a different angle. I twirled and faced the filing cabinets. If the initials stood for clients, we should have records of them.

I wheeled the chair to the last cabinet where we kept closed cases and tugged on a handle. Locked. Back at Maya's desk, I opened each drawer, searching for the tiny silver key. Gum, Chapstick, a movie theater stub, pens, notepad. Finally my fingers stumbled on a key. I unlocked the cabinet and stared at the manila files. The first time I'd combed through these, I'd been green. I recalled studying Derek's notes. How he hired actresses to help him catch his marks in the act. How he billed the wives. How long he was on stakeouts. I'd been in training mode then. I hadn't been vested in memorizing client names. It was unnecessary, since they were all closed cases anyway. But now I couldn't help but feel a nudge of guilt. What if I'd glossed over something that held the identity to Derek's shooter?

At the time, Derek had been working on the Booker case. I searched the files but there was no Booker listed in the B's. I sat back, my eyes roving the massive wall of files. I absently ran my hand over the ledger's smooth, leather cover. My wrist touched the cool, gold letters. Derek Matthew Bond. Or in this case, Derek Bond Matthew. Why was it custom practice to put the initial of the person's last name in the middle? That never made sense to me.

Something clicked. March thirtieth had listed ABM. Had Derek filed them in the same order? Something Booker something.

I hurried to the M's and there it was: Abigail Booker Marie.

I laughed loud. Derek's own filing system. Maybe he thought Big Brother could point their satellites through the front windows. I yanked Booker's file from the drawer. Okay, so who was RBS?

I had a suspicion, but I didn't want to get my hopes up until I found it. And there it was, all shiny and sparkling, at least in my mind. Rebecca *Bernstein* Susan.

I pulled the Bernstein file, my mind churning over just what this meant. Bernstein's wife had been one of Derek's clients. The same man Brady allegedly killed.

Funny Derek never mentioned *that* bit of info either.

I locked the cabinet, returned the key to Maya's drawer, and hurried into my office. I almost knocked my desk lamp onto the floor in my haste to turn it on. I sank into my chair and opened Bernstein's file first.

Mrs. Rebecca Susan Bernstein had hired Derek to follow her husband, Edward Daniel Bernstein, and discover if he was cheating. He'd been coming home later than usual, wasn't at the office when he said he was, and had become distant. It was a familiar story, one we heard a dozen times a year. Accordingly, Derek ran the usual surveillance and hadn't uncovered anything conclusive. There were no pictures in the file, however, just all handwritten notes.

I leaned back in my chair and shut my eyes, picturing when I first came on board. Derek had just gotten out of the hospital and was staying on the boat. I'd been more focused on his recovery, starting a new life, learning to keep the business afloat than investigating his shooting. I hadn't thought much of it at the time, but Derek had been largely uninterested in investigating it also. He'd assumed it was an unhappy client or spouse. Lord knew enough of them *wanted* to shoot the messenger. We just both assumed someone actually had.

At the time he'd said he only had two open cases. Booker and Anderson, some elderly couple. But it turned out that Mr. Anderson had been sneaking around with Mrs. Anderson's sister in order to plan a surprise birthday party for the wife. Everyone was happy, albeit not surprised, at the end. Booker had seemed the likely culprit.

Of course, he had failed to mention the Bernsteins.

I grabbed the Bernstein file again, flipping it open. Tons of notes, no pictures. Why? Where was all the surveillance that Derek had written about doing? Derek was a stickler for record keeping. If the photos were gone, it wasn't because they'd been misplaced. They'd been purged on purpose. Which in itself was enough to light a burning desire in my gut to see those pictures. Had Derek taken the photos? It was possible. It wasn't like I'd guarded our past client files in those early months of Derek teaching me the ropes. He'd been in and out of the office as much as the doctors would allow, and I wouldn't have looked twice at him leaving with a file under his arm.

Which meant if they did exist, they were on Derek's boat. Fat chance of getting to them there. Derek rarely left these days, and as tidy as his files were, clearly his home was not.

But there might be one other place I could see those pictures.

I glanced at the time. It was near eleven, and I had an appointment with Mrs. Martin at noon, according to the sticky note Maya had left on my desk. That meant my morning was free. According to the files in my hand, Mrs. Bernstein had lived in Brentwood at the time she'd hired Derek. If I was lucky, she might still live there. And she might still have copies of those pictures.

I switched off the light, stuffed the files into my purse, and locked up. Outside the temp had dropped a few degrees, but it was still hot enough to opt for air conditioning over throwing the top down on my convertible.

My phone vibrated as I got in. It had done that several times tonight. I hadn't checked who was calling, but I assumed it was Aiden. I was torn between ignoring the calls and wanting to hear his voice. Maybe I could steer the conversation away from court? Fat chance. When Aiden made his mind up, he didn't budge. A great lawyer trait, but not so great in the potential boyfriend department.

I slid behind the wheel and slammed the door shut. I tossed my purse onto the passenger seat and placed my cell in a cup holder, watching the display light up with Aiden's private cell phone number. I ignored it and pushed my key into the ignition.

But from the corner of my eye, I caught movement in the rear view mirror.

I looked up and gasped.

Jack Brady was in my backseat.

# CHAPTER NINE

———

Jack's eyes held that same cold, hard stare from the courtroom. He leaned forward slowly, as if he purposely wanted to threaten me. His approach worked. I reached for my purse, but it was too far from my grip. I'd taken my gun out of my holster and tossed it into my bag when I first got to the office. Instinct screamed for me to not make any sudden movements. I was pretty certain he could snap my neck like a chicken bone.

"What do you want?" I kept my voice at an even level. He didn't need to know my knees were shaking.

"Funny. That's my question to you. You come by my house, harass my girlfriend, and then show up in court. Who sent you?"

Did Jillian say I harassed her? She hadn't seemed overly upset at my questions, but then again, I had no idea how she'd presented them to Brady. I had a feeling Brady was about as sharp as he was menacing. It wouldn't take much to see through Jillian if he was already suspicious.

Or hiding something.

"I asked you a question." He hissed the words.

Goosebumps raised along my arms, but I refused to let him see my fear. "It's a public trial. The better question is, what the hell are you doing sneaking into my car?"

I tilted to my right, trying to discreetly grab my purse. He must've noticed my movement because he leaned all the way forward, his breath ruffling the hair next to my ear. It took all of my restraint not to gasp out loud. He raised his arms so they lay across the back of the seat, as if we were old friends just chatting about the past. In his right hand, he gripped a gun.

A delivery truck rattled by, and shouts echoed from

down the street. Perspiration pressed my blouse to my back.

"Stay out of my business. Do you understand?" he growled.

I should have nodded and agreed to his demands, but I didn't like being told what to do. "I won't stop looking for the truth about Derek."

He didn't make a sound, and from the mirror, I couldn't tell if he was seething or processing. Finally, he leaned even closer; his lips touched the back of my neck. It was an intimate move that felt all kinds of icky with a gun pressed to my side.

His breath whispered along my skin. "Then you're either stupid or you want to die."

My heart froze in my chest, time standing still for a moment at the threat I had a sinking feeling was not in any way idle.

Before I could react, however, the back door opened and a wave of warm air permeated the car. It slammed shut, and I exhaled. I twisted faster than a tornado and locked all the doors. I watched Brady glide across the street to his car, my heart racing in my chest now even though Brady appeared without a care in the world. As if he hadn't just waved a gun in my face and talked about my death.

Up until this point, I hadn't wanted to believe that Derek was really involved with someone like Brady. But the fact that Brady hadn't denied knowing Derek sealed it. He knew him. It was more than just the one drink the two men had shared. It was something big enough to make Brady threaten my life. I pressed my fingers to the spot on my neck where Brady's lips had been.

My phone buzzed, causing me to flinch. Without thinking, I snatched it out of the holder and pressed the green receiver button. "Aiden?"

He hesitated long enough for me to wonder if I'd lost the connection. "What's wrong?"

He could tell. Damn. My head swam with possible scenarios if I told him the truth. The worst being that Aiden would involve the police, Brady's bail would be revoked, and there went any chance I had of finding out what he had to do with Derek's shooting.

"Jamie, where are you? Are you okay?" Aiden's tone

went from concern to fear.

I turned the key in the ignition, hoping the roar of the engine would help me push some words out. "I'm fine. Just spooked."

"Why? Are you home or at the office?" His breathing came fast, as if he was running.

I glanced at the brick building and backed onto the street. I didn't want to stay here another minute. "I'm on my way home. It's not a big deal."

But it was. Despite this line of work, I've had a gun pointed at me only twice. A few months ago on another case that had gone horribly wrong and just now. Brady may have only meant to scare me, but the first time I'd been on the business end of a gun, I'd almost died. I wasn't particularly calm around bullets anymore.

"I'll meet you there."

I wanted to tell him no, that I didn't need his hand holding, but who was I kidding? Some hand holding, and maybe even some body holding, was exactly what I needed.

* * *

By the time Aiden arrived, I was already in my apartment, shoes kicked off and swallowing a fiery shot of tequila. I let him in, and the bottle of Cuervo was the first thing he noticed, his eyebrows furrowing in concern. The first thing *I* noticed, however, was the way his navy T-shirt hugged his biceps and chest. He was in jeans and sneakers, his hair still wet at the ends as if he'd called me fresh out of the shower.

"Hey," I said. Lame, but after a couple of shots, I wasn't a master conversationalist.

"Hey." Aiden stepped into the room and immediately cupped my jaw with his hands. His gaze roamed my face from forehead to chin several times, as if my worry lines were a map to my secrets. "Please tell me what has you so upset you're doing shots at midnight?"

I gulped, his hands warm and smelling like soap. It was nice. Comforting. Now that I was securely in my home, the immediate shock was wearing off, and I was able to deal better. I couldn't tell him the truth. In addition to my earlier reasons, I was a licensed PI. How would it look if I needed the Assistant District Attorney to save me? Who would hire the Bond Agency again? Plus, I would hate for Brady to think he won.

I rounded my shoulders and tried to shake any insecurities from my expression. "It was actually silly. Not a big deal, and I'm now ashamed that you drove all the way here for no reason."

Yes, the bullshitting was necessary to give me enough time to think up an appropriate and believable story. Man, I hated lying to him.

"What happened?"

I pointed to the bottle. "Do you want a drink?"

He dropped his hands and quirked a brow. He knew I was stalling. "No, I can't stay long. I have court in the morning."

I bit my lip. "Then I'm twice as sorry you came out here for no reason."

He narrowed his eyes, putting on the same penetrating look I'd seen earlier when he questioned the officer on the stand. "What happened, Jamie?"

I cleared my throat, looking down at the Cuervo to avoid his gaze. "I-I parked in the back corner of the lot beside the agency. When I went to my car, a man spooked me." There. Not a lie.

"Who was he?"

"Um, just a…homeless guy." Okay, so a little lie.

Aiden grabbed my hands. "Did he touch you, hurt you?"

"He didn't lay a finger on me." And technically, Brady hadn't. Just his lips.

Aiden let out a deep sigh, running a hand through his hair. He was really worried. Maybe it was the tequila working its way through my system, but I found the thought totally endearing. And kinda hot.

I stepped closer, catching a whiff of aftershave. "I'm sorry I made you rush over. You should be resting for tomorrow. You were excellent today."

He shook his head. "I got creamed. Not only did Wylie look like a puddle of sweat, Richmond also shredded my weapons expert, Dwyer."

So that's who had walked in as I hightailed it out. "How?"

"He kept objecting and commenting on how the gun didn't belong to Brady. Most of what he said was overruled, and even though the jury's directed to not pay attention, they still hear. You can't tell me they forget and ignore that information when it comes to decision time."

In the few months we've known one another, I'd come to associate Aiden with confidence. This uncertain side of him was something new. It left me with an instinctual urge to comfort him.

"I'm sure you've scored more points than you think."

He ran a hand through his hair again and stared off into space. "Yeah, maybe."

"You sure you don't want that drink?" I asked, holding up the Cuervo with a smile.

But instead of taking me up on the offer, Aiden turned his penetrating lawyer look on me again. "What was going on between you and Brady in the courtroom?"

I knew he'd get to that eventually, but it didn't stop me from cringing. I considered adding another lie to the mix, but I was tired. And he deserved more. "I spoke to his girlfriend to see if she knew anything about Derek's shooting."

His brows rose. "Did she?"

"No. It was a waste of time."

He held my gaze for a second, waiting for me to continue. When I didn't, he let his eyes wander over my place, as if finally seeing his surroundings. "This is the first time I've seen your apartment."

I waved a hand. "What do you think of my humble abode?"

"Nice. Cozy."

He was being polite. It was tiny. And with the minimal amount of time I spent in it, far from homey. But it did have one definite selling point.

"You haven't seen the best part yet." I parted the vertical blinds along the back wall. I didn't own the greatest furniture, second-hand pieces from estate sales, plus the occasional table from a discount store. But what my place lacked in decor, it made up for in view. The night shone with dotted lights of the Hollywood skyline below.

Aiden walked to my side. His shoulder brushed mine. "It's breathtaking."

"Yes." And I wasn't just referring to the view.

Here's the thing, between Aiden's sometimes stoic demeanor, our crazy schedules, and my occasional burst of playing hard-to-get, we had yet to cross that line from "will they, won't they?" to "my place or yours?" Our flirtatious Ping-Pong game left me confused, not quite sure whose side of the table the ball fell off last.

"I'd like to come back some evening when I can truly appreciate this," he said, as if reading my thoughts.

Maybe it was the tequila again, but I was feeling bold. I turned to him and placed a hand on his chest. I counted his heartbeats until he lowered his face to mine. One, two, three, four…

Then he leaned in, and his lips pressed against my forehead.

My forehead.

Are you kidding me? This is the kind of kiss you give your child…or dog.

When he straightened, he looked like he'd dozed off during that peck. His eyes were hooded, and I could swear he hid a yawn.

"I'm sorry. It's been a long day."

I bit the inside of my cheek. I wasn't sure if that was a brush off or his way of saying he was actually too exhausted to think of anything as aerobic as ripping each other's clothes off.

"Sure. Rain check," I said, hopefully doing a decent job of hiding my disappointment.

When we reached my door, he glanced back. "Hey, thanks for showing up in court today. I appreciate the support."

The look on his face was so genuine, my heart did a little flip in my chest. "Any time."

Which was another lie. There was no way I wanted to face Brady ever again, not even with a big, safe courtroom full of people between us.

* * *

The next morning, I stepped into a racer-back tank dress, a pair of pumps, and a loose cotton blazer. I added extra mascara to make up for the fact I'd spent another night tossing and turning, and hopped into my roadster, heading south on the 405 toward Brentwood. According to the county records I'd accessed after Aiden left, Mrs. Rebecca Bernstein *did* still own her home there. I hadn't seen Bernstein's wife in court yesterday, so I took a chance that she was staying home to avoid the media attention. I pulled up to the address and found a two-story brick structure with a semi-circular driveway and enough planted flowers to supply the Rose Parade. I parked by the front door. As I lifted the brass knocker I went through the different roles I could play to gain access. Reporter, one of Bernstein's old clients, a client's wife…but none seemed to fit. And since I hadn't had my daily dose of caffeine yet, I was cranky and simply tired of playing games.

The door opened, and a woman with dark hair and startlingly light green eyes greeted me. I recognized her face from the news articles I'd seen on the trial, but she was much more put together today than the grieving widow I'd seen depicted in the media. Her hair was pinned up into a bun, a single strand of pearls circled her neck, and she wore a simple floral, sleeveless dress. "Hello, may I help you?"

I extended my hand. "Hi, I'm Jamie Bond. I'm a private investigator with the Bond Agency."

Her eyebrows rose slowly. If I had to guess, their rise was impeded by Botox.

"Are you Mrs. Bernstein?" I pressed.

She nodded. "Yes, please come in." She stepped back and held the door open for me.

I entered and immediately my nose tickled. The air was heavy with perfume, as if she polished the wood with it. The foyer was grand yet simple at the same time. Light-colored walls with dark wood floors and moldings. The staircase semi-circled like the driveway and led to a second floor landing with a large bay window. The sunlight spilled onto the stairs and made diamond shaped beams by my feet. Bernstein must've done very well in life. According to Derek's file, he'd been a criminal attorney. I wondered what sort of clientele he'd defended.

"May I help you with something?" Mrs. Bernstein asked.

I smiled at her. "You hired Derek Bond a few years back?"

She motioned for me to follow her into a room to the right. "Yes. Are you related?"

The living room held the typical furnishings, all in muted shades of yellow and light blue. Every surface, including the floor before the great windows facing the front of the house, was lined with vases of flowers. Roses, daises, tulips, and ones I didn't know by name, in all colors.

"Yes. He's my father." I sat on the sofa.

She grinned. "He's a wonderful man."

I nodded, though I wasn't sure I believed her.

"May I get you some tea or coffee?" she offered.

I was so used to doors slamming in my face lately that her friendliness made me suspicious. But who was I to give up free caffeine? "Coffee would be great."

Her smile grew and she hurried off. I expected her to summon the help and put in our order, but I didn't hear any voices, just cupboard doors and the faucet turning on and off. Maybe it was the maid's day off. Surely Mrs. Bernstein didn't clean this place by herself. If she did, I needed to hire her. But the moment she spent away gave me enough time to admire her taste.

As well as snoop, of course.

There wasn't much personal material in this room, aside from several framed photographs stuck between vases. There was one of Mrs. Bernstein with a woman that resembled her. They were around the same age, so probably a sister. And the others were of small children. Since this didn't appear to be a house with scattered toys or the sounds and smells of little feet, I assumed they were nieces and nephews.

The wall above the fireplace had a large, lighter colored rectangle in the center. At first I thought it was the sunlight casting a shadow, but then I realized there must've been a picture there before. Perhaps a family portrait that had been removed after her husband's death.

Mrs. Bernstein returned with a tray of coffee and Danish. She set it on the table and handed me a cup. "There's cream and sugar. And please help yourself to a pastry. They're fresh from the bakery this morning."

"Thank you." A quick glance at my watch reminded me it was barely nine-thirty. I'd worried it was too early to visit, and she'd already been up and to the store.

"So how can I help you?" She dumped three spoonfuls of sugar in her dainty china cup then settled into an arm chair across from me.

"I was looking into some old cases and came across yours." It was a weak intro I knew. Who would be interested in her three-year-old file about a man who was deceased? I swallowed a large mouthful of coffee, and hoped my brain would kick in harder soon.

"Your father was a big help to me and my marriage."

"Oh?" I sipped my coffee again and let her talk.

"I was certain my husband, Edward…Eddie, was being unfaithful." Her eyes became moist. She grabbed a napkin and dabbed at their corners. "I'm sorry."

"Don't be." I sat back and hoped she'd continue.

"He's dead now. I'm sure you've heard about the trial. It's all over the news."

I nodded. "I have. I'm sorry. It must be difficult for you."

"Thank you. I know I should be in the courtroom, but I honestly just don't think I can face that man."

I noticed she didn't use Brady's name. "I understand," I told her, meaning it more than she knew.

"Anyway, um, what was I saying?" she asked, doing more eye-dabbing.

"You hired Derek to follow your husband?"

She nodded. "Right. Well, Eddie had started staying late at the office. Later than usual, I mean. His cell phone would ring, and he'd leave the room to talk, or would stop talking when I'd enter."

"That isn't usual for an attorney? They keep odd hours, have to maintain confidentiality?"

She rubbed her hand across her midsection. "Yes, but I knew in my gut that this was different. Or so I thought."

In my experience, the wife always knows. "So you hired Derek?"

"Yes, yes. He came highly recommended from a friend. But after a couple of weeks of following him around, your father concluded that Eddie was actually doing business and not having an affair." Her smile was as watery as her eyes.

"That's good."

She drew in a long breath. "Yes, I just wish I'd known sooner. Then we could've spent more quality time together before he was killed."

She felt guilty for suspecting him. Understandable. "Do you still have a copy of any photos or any tangible evidence that Derek gave you?"

She frowned. "No-no, he didn't show me anything. There wasn't anything to show."

Now it was my time to frown. Even when there's no evidence to support adultery, there's evidence to disprove it. Derek always gave photos to the wife. It was one of the first things he'd taught me.

So where were they?

# CHAPTER TEN

———

I left Mrs. Bernstein's and drove back to the agency, parking near the entrance. Top down today. I wasn't in the mood for any more surprise visitors in my backseat.

Maya was on the phone, as usual, but instead of giving me a wave as I walked by, she ignored me, a frown between her brows. Not that I expect to be greeted with cheers and excitement every time I entered the office, but I'd never known Maya to be distracted to the point of not handing me a stack of messages the second I walked through the door. She was shaking her head, biting her lip, clearly not liking whatever was being said on the other end of the phone.

I took slow steps toward my office, lingering in hopes of catching a snippet of her conversation. Yes, being nosy was not only a part of my job description, but my nature.

As I reached my door, I heard her say, "Yeah, Mom, I know how important it is to you. I'll try to make it, but work is really busy."

I waited until Maya hung up, then turned and walked back to her desk. "Is everything alright?"

She flinched and widened her eyes. "Sorry, boss. I didn't see you walk in."

"I noticed. That phone call seemed intense."

She pushed a lock of her dark hair behind an ear, grabbing a stack of pink papers and handing me my messages. "It's my mother," she explained, "and her bi-monthly Vagina Meeting."

I blinked. "Excuse me?"

She rolled her eyes. "My mother, Charlotte Emily Alexander—named after the Bronte sisters—lost my father six years ago, and since that time she's gone from a hopeless romantic to a feminist who holds luncheons disguised as discussions on how men suck. The only problem is she still believes the man should pay the check while the woman just looks pretty. She's a walking oxymoron."

I tried not to smile. "And she wants you to attend?"

"Oh, no. She expects it. And in the midst of the man-hating, the conversation always circles around to how sexist my *Playboy* spread was and what self-respecting man will want to marry a girl who showed that much skin." She cocked a brow before I had time to comment. "Not directly, but in gist. I usually screen my calls every other Monday, but I got careless and picked up today. Big mistake."

I felt for her. Most of the time, I did the same with Derek. Lately, I understood complicated parent-child relationships as well as anyone. "Sorry," I said, laying a hand on her arm.

Maya shrugged. "I'll live. I just may need to drink heavily afterward, so if I call in sick with a hang-over tomorrow, you know why."

"Listen, let me go with you," I heard myself offering on impulse.

She paused. "Seriously?"

"Sure. I mean, it's a free lunch, right?"

Maya grinned. "Now there's looking at the silver lining. But, really, I can't ask you to do that."

I waved her off. "What are friends for? Besides," I said, talking myself into it as much as Maya now, "who doesn't enjoy an afternoon of good old fashioned man-bashing?" I asked. I was only half joking. There was more than one man making my life difficult at the moment.

"Thank you, Jamie. This means a lot." She scribbled her mother's address on a Post-it and handed it over. "One-thirty. Cool?"

I nodded, glancing at the clock. It was coming on noon now, which left me just enough time to run one errand before the luncheon. "I'll be there."

"And I promise, if it gets unbearable we'll leave," Maya reassured me.

I smiled, not sure what to say to that, and headed to my

office. I tossed my purse into my desk drawer and checked the stack of messages. A couple of clients looking for progress reports, a lawyer wanting to clarify some points about our surveillance before a divorce hearing, a couple of prospective new clients looking to schedule consultations. I was about to call the lawyer back when Danny appeared in my office doorway.

I paused, phone in hand. I hadn't seen him since he'd been in the buff at the resort. For that matter, I had been, too.

He waved at me. I waved back, sure my cheeks were getting hot at the memory.

"Uh, hey, thank you for helping us out yesterday," I said, setting my phone down. "You know, at the nudist colony," I added. Then suddenly felt ridiculous for pointing out the nude thing again.

"Any excuse to get naked with you, James." He grinned.

I blushed deeper, sure I was positively crimson. "Right." I cleared my throat. "Good times."

His grin grew wider, and he leaned in as if sharing a secret. "You're thinking about me naked right now, aren't you?"

"No!" I made a pfft sound, expelling air through my teeth. "Totally not."

His grin was practically taking over his entire face. "Really? Because I'm totally thinking about you naked."

If the earth could have swallowed me up right then, I would have been eternally grateful. My cheeks were on fire, my gaze pinging anywhere but at Danny.

"Relax, Bond. I'm teasing you," he said, taking a step forward. "Besides, I've seen far more of you on location."

I gasped. "You did not! When?"

"In Brazil, Cabo, New Zealand...take your pick."

I shook my head. "I was always dressed."

"But those bikinis were so tiny, they didn't hide much."

"*Much* being the operative word."

Danny smiled again, showing off the impish dimple in his left cheek. "Okay, I lied. Yesterday was the first time I've seen you naked, and, damn you're hot, girl. Feel better?"

Hardly. The heat in my cheeks started pooling into that southern region again, making me oddly uncomfortable. Danny was my best friend. Friends did not comment on how hot their naked friends were.

And said friends weren't supposed to be turned on by it.

I cleared my throat. "Why are you here, exactly?" I asked.

"I wanted to take you to lunch. I thought meatball subs felt like the perfect way to celebrate a case closed."

I bit my lip. Meatball subs sounded like heaven right now. "Actually, I already have plans."

His grin faltered. "You do?"

I shrugged. "Sorry. I'm a popular girl."

"These plans wouldn't have anything to do with a certain ADA, would they?"

Did I detect just the slightest note of jealousy there?

I opened my mouth to respond, but before I could, my phone beeped and Maya's voice filled the room. "Mrs. Martin's here to see you."

"Sorry. Gotta go," I said, gesturing to the door.

Danny nodded, backing out of my office. "Sure. Right. See you later," he said, heading into the lobby. I saw him stop by Maya's desk, no doubt trying to get info from her on just who my lunch date was. I could have told him it was Maya herself, but considering the way he'd just teased me, I figured it was payback to let him think the worst for a bit.

I hurried to my desk, and clicked the intercom button on the phone. "Send her in, Maya."

Mrs. Martin shuffled in, bags under her eyes, shoulders slumped. I could tell she wasn't looking forward to whatever I had to say. She slowly sat in a chair facing my desk. "Your associate called and said you have information. He's cheating, isn't he?"

I couldn't tell if her edgy tone was from relief that she'd soon be free of the adulterer or horrified that he was actually cheating. Some wives, even though they knew the truth in their gut, couldn't quite believe it when shown the proof. Or didn't want to.

I sat in my chair and placed a hand on her folder. "We've discovered behavior that leads us to believe that your husband might be unfaithful."

She stared at me, her expression blank. The first time I'd

met her, she wore a tailored suit with flawless makeup and her hair spun up into a classic updo. Today, she wore Mom jeans, a cotton-knit top, and flip-flops. Her hair was down, pulled behind her ears, but it looked frizzy and unwashed. When she snapped out of it, her voice was calm and steady. "Show me."

My gut tensed, but I opened the folder and pulled out three photographs of Martin squeezing various parts of Caleigh's anatomy. I slid them toward the wife and bit my bottom lip, hoping she wouldn't start crying. I hated the tears.

Mrs. Martin's hand trembled as she held the pictures. She squeezed her eyes shut and laid the photos back on my desk. When she opened them, she stared directly at me. "I guess I shouldn't be surprised. I did hire you, after all. I knew he wasn't an angel. But I just kind of hoped I was being paranoid..." She trailed off, eyes cutting to the photos again.

"I'm sorry," I told her, truly meaning it. "If there's anything I can do?"

She shook her head, gathering up the photos and shoving them into her purse. "No. Thank you. You've done enough. Just...send me a bill, okay?"

I nodded. "Of course." I stood to walk her out. We passed through the lobby, conversation between Maya and Danny immediately ceasing in deference to what they knew she'd just seen.

"Again, please let me know if there's anything else we can do for you," I added as Mrs. Martin hit the door.

She started to shake her head, then paused. "Actually, do you know if my husband is still at the resort?"

"I, uh..." I looked to Danny. He'd been the last one to see Martin. He gave me a quick nod. "Yes, as far as I know, he's still there."

Mrs. Martin gave me a tight smile. "Thank you," she said, then turned and walked quickly out the door and down the carpeted hallway.

I stood in the doorway watching her go. Gone was the slumped-shouldered look, and in its a place a brisk walk that I could swear was suddenly full of determination.

I quickly turned back to the lobby.

"Maya!"

She bounced up from her spot behind the desk. "Yeah, boss?"

"We ran a background check on Mrs. Martin, didn't we?" Ever since that past case of mine had gone bad, landing me in Aiden's courtroom, we had a strict policy of screening clients. We checked IDs thoroughly, went through financials, made sure no one involved had a violent criminal record.

Maya nodded. "Of course. She came up clean. Not even a parking ticket." She paused. "Why?"

I bit my lip. "I don't know. She just seemed…" I trailed off, not able to put the uneasy feeling growing in the pit of my stomach into words. "Is Caleigh still at the resort?" I asked.

"I, uh, I don't know. I mean, I think she spent the night, but I'm not sure if she's headed back yet."

"Find out. And, if she is there, tell her to stay awhile longer and keep an eye on Mr. Martin."

"What's wrong?" Danny asked, a frown between his brows. "You think the wife is going to pull something?"

I shook my head. "No. Probably not. I hope not."

"But better safe than sorry," Danny finished for me.

I nodded. "She seemed pretty upset."

"Okay, I'll go watch Caleigh's back," he offered.

"Oh, you don't have to—" I started.

But Danny cut me off, raising a palm my way. "Look, if the wife really is going to go all bunny-boiling, I don't want Caleigh up there alone."

He had a good point. "Thank you," I told him, suddenly reminded of just why he'd been my best friend for so long. He could go from lustful, sexual innuendo to knight in shining armor in seconds flat. But the truth was, in a clinch, I had a feeling he was 90% knight and only 10% lust.

"No sweat," he said. "Hey, I can think of worse ways to spend the afternoon than naked among a bunch of lonely women."

Okay, maybe 20% lust.

* * *

Maya's mother lived in the suburb of Downey, just

southeast of Los Angeles. I parked on the edge of the driveway, my backside almost sticking out into the road. Two other cars were parked ahead of me, and I saw Maya's Jetta slide to a stop at the curb. I stepped out, slammed the door shut, and Maya was instantly at my side.

"Thank you again for doing this," she said as we walked past an angry looking garden gnome.

"No problem." On the drive over, I'd geared myself up for an intellectual conversation about equality in the workplace and female reproductive rights. With that came images of drinking tea from bone china while nibbling on crustless sandwiches, gathered around a Victorian-laced coffee table on a hard settee. I hadn't expected a sunny bungalow with stained-glass windows and a walkway lined with potted plants.

The one-story house was small, on a crowded street of other small homes. Unlike Mrs. Bernstein's or most of our clients' homes, the Alexander neighborhood looked homey. A tricycle sat on the grass of the house to the left. A stray baseball had landed in Maya's mother's yard. Maya picked it up and gently tossed it over. It landed with a soft thud beside the bike. A white wicker armchair stood close to the front door, where a wooden plaque, painted in bright yellow, declared this as being: The Alexander Home. Beneath the childlike lettering were three stick figures, each one labeled. Robert, Charlotte, Maya.

It made my throat constrict. Partly because Maya's father was gone, and partly because I didn't own anything from my life with my mother. Everything had been sold, donated, or given away, Derek wanting to purge the place of bad memories. There were a few items that I'd tucked away, but they'd either been broken or lost over time.

I barely had time to cross the Welcome mat when three older women came to the door to greet us. Mrs. Alexander, who insisted I call her Charley, plus her two "dearest friends in the whole wide world," Ruth and Abigail. They each wore the same sundress but in a different color: yellow, light blue, and peach respectively. Their outfits were completed with white open-toed sandals, matching pedicures, and silver hoop earrings. Charley wore her hair up in a bun, while the other two pulled theirs back into loose braids.

The women were much older than I expected, early sixties easily. Charley must've had Maya in her late thirties, at least. Which wasn't uncommon now, but was considered later in life for Charley's generation. I wondered why she'd waited. Had she been a career woman or just late to find love in Maya's father? It made me realize I knew precious little about Maya's personal life. She'd never spoken much of her family, and I hadn't even realized her father was deceased until she'd mentioned it this afternoon.

The ladies led me into a small formal dining room with a table eclectically set for six. It looked like a child's tea party with orange, yellow and blue tableware and clear vases filled with blue and green glass beads. I half expected Baby Alive or Raggedy Ann to be seated amongst us.

Charley took my arm and guided me to a chair to the right of hers, which was at the head of the table. "Please make yourself comfortable. *Mi casa es su casa.*"

"Very good, Mom." Maya looked to me. "She's been studying languages at the college. She's on Spanish now."

"Yes, I started with French. Very classy. *J'adore tes chaussures.*"

"She loves your shoes," Maya interpreted. "I took French in high school, and shoes was the first word I learned." She grinned. A girl after my own heart.

I glanced at my leopard-skin pumps. "Thank you. Um...*merci.*" I hoped it would end there because I spent my high school Spanish days flirting with the boys, and my French was rustier than that.

Ruth and Abigail, who settled across from me and Maya, cheered like I'd just pulled a Frenchman from my purse.

I nodded to Maya about the sixth setting at the other side of the table. Were we waiting for another friend?

Maya leaned close. "She likes to put out a place for Dad."

A breath swelled in my chest. How sad.

Charley removed the lids from three serving platters, with the theatrical flourish of a magician on stage. She even did a "ta-da" each time. With each discovery, Ruth and Abigail again cheered. While I recognized the flatbread, I wasn't sure what the others were, but they smelled spicy and earthy. My stomach grumbled.

"Mom's been taking a tour of the world in her cooking class," Maya said. "Where are you now, Mom?"

"India. The first is Tandoori Chicken. I use boneless breast meat because I prefer bite-size pieces. It has yogurt and garlic and tandoori spices, of course."

Of course. She must've had a lot of time on her hands.

"The next one is Palak Paneer." She smiled after she said the name with a pseudo Indian accent. "Abigail is vegetarian, so there always must be one meatless dish. This one is spinach and paneer cheese, which I made from scratch."

Ruth clapped.

Charley gave a half bow. "And the last is Naan, which you can use to scoop up all the deliciousness of the other two. Please help yourselves."

Everyone became busy with serving themselves and passing around the dishes. A flurry of cumin, coriander, and ginger tickled my nose. Not exactly a summertime menu. I expected cucumber sandwiches and iced tea, but the house was so well air-conditioned that it was almost chilly, so hot, spicy food hit the spot.

"So, Jamie, Maya tells us you track down adulterers, "said Ruth between bites.

I nodded. "It's a living."

"No details," Maya quickly added.

All three women widened their eyes and shook their heads. "Oh no."

I shoved a piece of chicken into my mouth, and immediately washed it down with water. The spices clawed at my throat at first, but once they went down, it left a lingering warmth in my belly.

"How very independent of you to manage your own agency," said Charley.

"I don't do it alone. I have Maya and the other girls." I paused, remembering the feminist company I was keeping. "Er, women, I mean. But Maya's a tremendous support. She practically runs the place."

Ruth and Abigail beamed. Charley glanced from me to

her daughter, expressionless. I wasn't sure if she was pondering what I said or finding a tactful way to disagree. Did she only see Maya as the March Playmate or was she aware of her organizational skills?

"She's a receptionist. There's nothing wrong with that, dear, but answering phones isn't the same as being an entrepreneur."

Maya sighed. Not too loud, but I heard it.

"Being an *administrative assistant*, especially to a PI firm, isn't just about getting coffee. Which I couldn't live without, by the way, so she's basically saving my life on a daily basis."

Ruth and Abigail chuckled at my joke. Charley, not so much.

"Maya holds the rest of us together," I continued. "Without her attention to detail and her organization, we'd be lost. She handles every administrative aspect of every case we get. Without her, the agency wouldn't be half what it is now."

Maya's cheeks stained pink, and she looked away. I hoped she realized I was being truthful, even if I was laying it on a bit thick for her mother's benefit.

Charley cupped my hand and squeezed. "I'm thrilled she has such a magnificent boss."

"Thank you. But I'm thrilled to have such a great employee."

Charley made a grunting sound in her throat, but I couldn't tell if it was agreeing or disagreeing with me.

"It must be so exciting to spy on people," Abigail said.

I chuckled. "It can be."

"You're like Maddie from *Moonlighting*. Remember her with that handsome Bruce Willis, Charley?"

"No, no," said Ruth. "Jamie's more like Laura Holt with that hot Remington Steele."

I nearly choked on my paneer. If only my life was that adventurous.

"Do you have a Remington in your life, Jamie?" Ruth asked.

The three women simultaneously stopped eating and stared at me. Talk about a hot seat. My temperature rose, and I wasn't sure if it was the tandoori or the women.

"I-um…" I thought of Aiden. He was definitely close to Remington. But then Danny floated into my mind. Why, I have no idea except the haphazard feeling I got around him lately reminded me of Maddie and David Addison.

"I'm not sure. My love life is a bit complicated at the moment." And in all honestly, practically non-existent.

Ruth heavily sighed. "I do understand."

Abigail rolled her eyes.

My phone buzzed.

I glanced at the display. Danny. Oddly enough, I felt myself blush that I'd just been thinking of him.

"Uh, if you'll excuse me, I really have to take this."

Charley waved me on. "I understand. You're a career woman. Work has to come first."

I stabbed the on button as I walked into the living room, just out of earshot. "Hey, what's up?" I asked.

"Well, you were right," he told me. "The wife visited Martin here."

I felt my stomach instantly seize with dread. "And? Is he okay?"

"Okay is a relative term."

I closed my eyes and thought a really dirty word. "What did she do?"

"Apparently she caught up with Martin by the pool. Caleigh was with him, of course, but she said Mrs. Martin was calm, cool as a cucumber, didn't even show that she knew Martin was being unfaithful."

I felt the dread ease, glad I'd had Caleigh stick around.

"In fact," Danny went on, "Mrs. Martin went so far as to buy her husband a drink before leaving."

"So everything's fine?" I asked. Why did I get the feeling that Danny was holding something back?

"It was. Caleigh watched Mrs. Martin leave, then stuck around a little while longer to make sure she didn't come back all psycho."

"She didn't, did she?"

"Nope. So, Caleigh she figured it was cool to start heading out herself. She went back to her room, packed up her things, and checked out of the resort. She was just about to go, when she spotted him."

"Spotted who? Martin?" I asked, getting that uneasy feeling again.

"Yep. Still at the pool. Two hours later."

"And?" What was he getting at?

"Mr. Martin was fast asleep. Sedative. Caleigh said she should have realized it when he downed the drink his wife gave him and immediately started yawning. He was asleep in the sunshine the whole time. And apparently Mr. Martin wasn't wearing any sunscreen."

My phone beeped, signaling that Danny had just sent me a photo message.

"You gotta see this, Bond," he said, the chuckle in his voice unmistakable before he hung up.

I tapped the screen, bringing up Danny's message. It was all I could do not to burst out laughing as I held the phone closer to my face to make out the picture.

Danny had photographed the man asleep on his lounge chair, on his back, in the blaring sun. His skin was the color of rubies. *Everywhere.* Score one for the wife. Mr. Martin wouldn't be bringing his little Mr. Martin out to play for a long time.

# CHAPTER ELEVEN

———

After the afternoon at Charley's, I spent a riveting evening with the three B's. My bathtub, a bottle of bubbles, and a couple of beers. Now, completely rested, at least physically, I sat in my car, parked diagonally from Derek's boat. I chose to hide beside a white Suburban, so he wouldn't see me, but I could barely see the dock. There was just enough space to make out Candy and Apple climbing onto his vessel. They were the errand I had quickly made before meeting Maya at her Mom's.

When I had arrived at The Spotted Pony, a gentleman's club in Burbank, the exotic dancers were in the dressing room, applying fake lashes and moisturizing their legs with glitter butter. They said it bounced off the stage lights, making their skin look shiny and touchable. Like the patrons needed the incentive. The girls, who had played a small role in some of my past investigations, had agreed to help me without hesitation. I loved that kind of enthusiasm. I told them where to go, instructing them to wait until they got my text. I'd wanted to make sure that Elaine was out of the picture tonight. As soon as I'd pulled up and seen her Honda missing, I'd texted them the go-ahead. Luckily, they hadn't disappointed, showing up twenty minutes later in smoking hot booty shorts and tight tanks that showed off their...assets.

I pulled a stick of gum out of my cup holder, popped the minty rectangle into my mouth, and rolled the foil into the tiniest square, flinging it back into the holder. How long would it take to convince Derek to go off with them? Hopefully not long. They had everything he loved most in women—double D's, skimpy clothes, and long legs. He couldn't resist. Right?

I strummed my fingers on the steering wheel to some

silent tune in my head. I glanced at my phone. Five minutes. I considered passing the time by catching up on my Angry Birds or an intellectual game of Word Whomp, but I didn't want to miss seeing them leave.

My phone rang. I glanced at the display. Danny. I clicked the button. "Hey, what's up?"

"I was calling to ask you the same. Thought I'd redeem myself after being shot down at lunch and maybe we could grab a late dinner? Whatever you're in the mood for."

"Actually," I said, glancing at the boat. "I'm kind of tied up tonight."

"Oh." Danny paused. "You do mean that figuratively, right? I mean, I'm not interrupting anything kinky right now, am I?"

I rolled my eyes. "Get your mind out of the gutter, Danny."

"Now what fun would that be?"

"I'm alone. I'm…working a case."

"Want a hand? Two heads are always better than one."

A lump settled in my throat. This was the first time I'd worked on a case without Danny or the girls. It felt odd. And lonely.

But I shook my head in the darkness. "No. Thanks, but this one is…kind of delicate."

I heard Danny nodding his head on the other end. "Gotcha. You working a skittish mark?"

He had no idea. I watched the *Black Pearl* sway on the dark water. "Very skittish." My gum had lost its flavor already, and I spat it out my window then grimaced at my littering.

"Well, listen, what's your schedule like tomorrow?" Danny asked.

I leaned back on my headrest, trying to remember the details Maya had thrust at me as we'd left her Mom's.

"I've got a new client meeting in the morning."

"Another cheating husband? You're lucky guys can't keep it in their pants."

I hated to admit that he was right. A boat horn honked out in the distance, but it was loud enough to echo across the phone line.

"Where are you?" Danny asked.

Damn.

"I'm...near the pier. Santa Monica," I lied. I bounced my right foot, making the car shake. I stared at Derek's boat, willing the three of them to come out.

"Oh. Well, let me know if you have some time tomorrow to grab a bite."

That was the third time in twenty-four hours Danny had suggested as much. Maybe it was the circumstance, or maybe the fact I'd just hired two strippers to lure my own father away from his boat for an hour, but suspicion was my first instinct. "Why are you so anxious to share a meal with me?" I asked.

"No reason," Danny said quickly. Too quickly.

"Don't bullshit me, Danny."

I heard a muted chuckle in response. "Okay, fine. There's...something I want to talk to you about. But it's nothing. It can wait," he covered quickly.

I felt an odd, squirmy feeling in my stomach, like whatever Danny wanted to talk about was the opposite of how unimportant he was making it seem. And a conversation I wasn't sure I wanted to have with him. I was about to come up with a fabulous excuse to put it off when a long leg emerged onto the top deck of Derek's boat. I held my breath. For a fleeting moment, I saw only the leg and thought of dismembered body parts, as if Derek had finally cracked from too much battery-acid coffee and motion sickness, and he'd chopped up the strippers. Clearly I needed to cut down on my reruns of *Criminal Minds*. But then a torso accompanied the legs—plural—and I sucked in a lungful of salty sea air. Candy. She wore a huge smile, and her top was a bit twisted. He didn't dare...

What was I thinking? The whole purpose of asking these women to help was because Derek, like the other men Danny had referenced, couldn't keep it in his pants.

"Jamie, you still there?"

Derek appeared next, with Apple at his heels.

Gotcha.

"Yeah, I'll call if I get a free minute tomorrow."

"Sure. Maybe we can do an early dinner."

"Maybe." I wasn't paying attention to what Danny was

saying anymore. I had no idea how Candy and Apple had lured Derek out, what they'd promised, or where they were going. And thankfully so, since I wanted to keep my Indian fare down, but that also meant I didn't know how long I had to snoop.

"I gotta go." I clicked off my phone and scooted down in my seat, keeping my head up at eye level, just enough to watch. Derek and the women walked along the dock, to Apple's car—a Granny Smith green Volvo. I'd expected she'd be more of a McIntosh or Red Delicious kinda girl. Derek kept one hand on each of their asses. Classy, Dad. They all moved in one fluid motion, like dance steps rehearsed ahead of time. The girls appropriately giggled at whatever he said, which probably wasn't truly funny. He never looked my direction.

Derek pulled up the backseat for Candy to scoot in, then folded his tall frame into the tiny car. Apple slid into her side, and after another round of high-pitched squeals, they pulled out of the marina.

I counted to ten, grabbed my phone, and stepped from my car.

Show time.

* * *

Once I was on Derek's boat, I started in his bedroom. It seemed the most likely place to hide things. I began with the obvious, the closet, and kept my eye on the time. I couldn't get caught, and there are only so many places to hide on a boat.

I combed through his clothes and a few boxes of crap— ratty T-shirts from bands I'd never heard of, a small stash of old records and odd knickknacks, like a porcelain duck wearing a raincoat and a mood ring way too small for his beefy fingers. I was starting to wonder if he was a closet hoarder. I then searched through his makeshift nightstand, which consisted of a cardboard box full of magazines and DVDs, beneath a three-legged table.

Yes, I'd found my father's porn collection. Yay me. Now I just needed to make an appointment with my shrink.

The dresser was the most uneventful container, clothes stuffed haphazardly in every drawer. Bedroom a bust, I ransacked the kitchen/galley, and other than a carton of cigarettes that he was supposed to have thrown out, there was nothing about any cases.

I was running out of time and patience. I headed to the bunks that served as his spare bedroom and bit my lip. If there was nothing here then what would be my next step? Fall to my knees and beg for answers? Not my style. I could bug his place, but it was highly unlikely that he'd suddenly start talking about a three-year-old case, and, even if he did, who would he discuss it with? Certainly not Elaine, Candy, or Apple. And as much as I knew Derek was lying and hiding something big, I couldn't stoop to that. He was my father. And there were certain things he did in private that I wanted to remain private.

The closet beside the bunks was empty except for a plush, white robe. There was no room for a dresser or night stand here. The area was devoid of anything but a bed, and a framed oil panting of a mountain under a sunny sky on the opposite wall. I sat on the twin-sized mattress as the boat rocked and almost tossed me into the back wall. Other than my rare occasional crashing here, I doubted anyone else ever slept here. Derek's house guests were usually of the share-the-bed-with-him variety.

The boat rocked again, sliding me toward the center of the bed. The back of my pump hit the wood platform beneath the mattress. The trundle.

I took in a sharp breath.

This was a trundle bed. That meant it had a drawer.

I slid off, onto my knees, and gripped the indentation in the mahogany wood. I pulled the bottom panel forward, and the drawer slid with ease. No mattress. Instead, Derek had used the drawer to house folders and a small box. It was as if the angels were singing, a rainbow descended over the boat, and this was my pot of gold.

I scanned the folders first. Names I didn't recognize. One contained a copy of my birth certificate and a picture of Derek and Mom holding me when I was first born. Their smiles were huge, proud. It brought a lump to my throat. I was tempted to swipe it, but I didn't want Derek to know I'd been here. Plus, I had a feeling it might be the only photo of Mom that he'd kept, the rest having been purged when she died. I set it aside and kept looking. I found Derek's birth certificate and his passport. It was old and expired. I wasn't aware of him ever leaving the country, yet it was stamped "London" about eight years ago, for a couple of weeks. I briefly wondered what he'd been doing there.

The folders a bust, I opened the box. I sucked in a breath. Inside were surveillance pictures, and on top of them was a lined sheet of paper with Derek's scrawl. It simply said: Bernstein. The angels went up an octave.

My phone buzzed, scaring the crap out of me. I glanced at it. Candy.

Her text read: *Couldn't hold him.*

Damn. They hadn't been gone that long, which meant he could be back any minute.

If he returned before I had time to get to my car, I couldn't get caught with pictures in my hands. I hadn't brought my purse, and my skirt and blouse left little space to hide objects, especially eight-by-tens. I grabbed my phone and clicked the button for the camera. I'd have to settle for pictures of pictures.

I zoomed in on the door of a building, time and date stamped a week before Bernstein was shot. I tried to decipher where they were, but I'd have to focus later.

Click, click. The first few came out too bright. I flipped through the settings on my phone, turning off the flash.

Perspiration built up on my forehead and the back of my neck. There wasn't time for this.

I retook those photos, noticing the better quality, and picked up the next one.

As I clicked the shutter on the last picture, the heavy fall of footsteps thudded above.

My heart leapt into my throat.

I shoved the photos back into the box. The corners of several bent, and they were in such disarray that I knew if Derek opened it, he'd know someone had been here. I pulled the photos back out and tapped them on the lid of the box, trying to slide them into a neat stack. One of them sliced my index finger.

Shit.

Paper cuts, even if it was photo-thick quality paper, stung like hell. I didn't have time to nurse it though.

I grabbed the box and something slid into its corner. A memory card. On instinct, I grabbed it, then gently placed the photos back in, and put everything back into the drawer.

Clutching the evidence in my hands, I stood, unsure where to go. I jerked back and forth for a second. I had no pockets.

The footsteps grew closer. Another minute, and he'd be climbing aboard.

I stuffed the memory card into my bra, and ran toward the galley, listening intensely to the footsteps.

They slowed and I froze, slamming into a wall. I didn't want him to hear me running and my pumps made a loud click-clack across the floor.

When he resumed, so did I.

I spotted his sneakers on the top step as I turned the corner. The boat swayed, and I dove into the bathroom, praying that wasn't his first stop. I'd just pulled the door shut, keeping a scant inch of space for me to peek out, and saw Derek's lumbering frame come into view.

I held my breath, sure that the rapid beat of my heart was loud enough to give me away.

Derek walked into the galley and grabbed a beer from the fridge. He sat at the table, and I prayed he wasn't settling in for a long night of drinking. The galley had a clear shot of the door. No way could I escape. He stared out the window, did some more drinking, then more staring. Just as my legs were starting to cramp, he mercifully got up and walked to the counter again. He dropped his beer can in the garbage, then picked up his cell. I watched him dial as he leaned against the counter, and I prayed like hell he wasn't calling me. He put the phone to his ear, waited as it rang on the other end (thankfully *not* in my hand), then finally say, "Hey, babe. It's me."

He paused, I assumed listening to the "babe" on the other end.

"Well, what are you doing tonight?" Pause. "Yeah, I know I said I needed some space, but…" Derek glanced out the window at the ocean again. "I'm lonely."

It was his classic booty-call line, but something about the empty look in Derek's eyes made me believe he was actually telling the truth.

"Yeah, I know you've got work in the morning," he said into the phone again. More pausing. "Well, I could drive you." Pause. "Twenty minutes?" Pause. "Perfect." Derek smiled, showing off his teeth in the dim light. "Can't wait. See you then, Elaine."

So Elaine was "babe." I wasn't surprised that he'd given her his needing-space line. I'd overheard it countless times during my teen years when his flavor of the month had started losing her luster. But I'd honestly never heard him call a woman back after his famous last line. Elaine really might be becoming a permanent fixture around here.

Derek hung up the phone, then disappeared into the bedroom. I heard drawers opening as he changed for his date.

I didn't waste a second, taking my heels off and slipping out the door and up the stairs. I tiptoed off the boat, cringing with every little creak of the ancient planks, then full-on sprinted back to my car, my stolen evidence jiggling in my D cups.

* * *

My cell rang as I kicked my apartment door shut. The display read: Aiden Prince. I raised an eyebrow. It was late. After midnight. Don't tell me the ADA did booty calls, too? I dropped my purse to the floor with a thud and pushed the on button.

"Hello?" I said. Which, in hindsight, might have been just a little breathless considering the adrenalin rush I'd been on.

"Wow, sexy. I wasn't prepared for that."

Warmth shot into my cheeks. "Well, I guess I'm just glad it's you," I quickly covered.

"I'm going to have to call you more often, then."

I pulled the memory card from my bra, set it on my coffee table and kicked off my shoes. "So what are you up to this evening, Mr. Prince?"

"I'm in bed. I mean, well…I'm going to sleep. Soon." He chuckled. "That sounded completely suggestive, didn't it?"

"Completely," I agreed, not able to keep the smile off my face.

"I didn't mean it that way. I just…wanted to hear your

voice before the day was over."

I felt a warm sensation spread through my chest. Suggestive and sweet in the same sentence. It would be so easy to fall for this guy. "Well, here it is," I told him.

He chuckled softly again, sending goosebumps all over my body. "How was your day, Jamie?"

"It went okay. Closed a case, did a luncheon." Broke into my father's boat, ransacked his personal space. "You? How was court?"

"Not much different than yesterday. So, you closed the nudist thing. Was he cheating?"

He didn't want to talk about court. I couldn't blame him. I didn't want to think about Brady. "Yep. But the wife got the last laugh," I told him, relaying the fate of poor sunburned Mr. Martin.

"Good for her," he said, laughing when I'd finished. Then he paused a moment. "You busy for lunch tomorrow?"

I bit my lip. That was two offers in one night. If I wasn't careful, the male attention was going to go to my head. "What do you have in mind?"

"I'd love to cash in on that rain check you owe me."

My cheeks warmed again. I felt the huge, cheesy smile spread on my face. "Just say where and when."

He named a place and time, and I felt myself nodding. "Looking forward to it. 'Night, Aiden."

"Good night, Jamie."

We clicked off, and I sat there, staring up at the ceiling for a few minutes, replaying our conversation and feeling like a giddy teenager with puppy love. Then my eyes strayed down to the card on my coffee table, snapping me back to reality.

I grabbed my laptop and phone and sat at my small dinette set. As the computer buzzed to life, I plugged the USB cord from my phone into the laptop and slipped the memory card into the reader.

The window for the pictures I'd copied came up first. It was some random building at night. A corner street lamp added some light to the location, as well as the interior overheads that spilled outside onto the concrete. Probably where Bernstein had worked—his law office. No people. Nothing of any use.

I minimized the window and pulled up a video from the memory card. I clicked play and watched the same building fill my screen. Same time of day. Great, another dead end.

But this time there was movement.

The front doors pushed out, and a young man stepped through them. He wore low-hanging jeans, sneakers, and a brown leather bomber jacket. He leaned against the brick structure and lit a cigarette. If I had to guess, I'd say he looked more like a client of Bernstein's than someone who worked in the expensive building. Derek zoomed the camera in, and I could make out the stubble on the young man's chin and a small teardrop tattoo near his eye. He couldn't be more than twenty, his eyes popping back and forth in his skull like Ping-Pong balls, his skin pitted. Gang for sure. Meth head likely.

He took two more drags then crushed the cigarette beneath his foot, turning to his left to do so. Some kind of graphic was etched onto the back of his jacket. I couldn't make out the whole thing, but it looked like an animal's face. Maybe a lion.

A car's motor was heard, and the guy looked to the street.

Derek zoomed out.

A blue sedan had pulled up in front, keeping its lights on and motor running. I stared at the driver. His head was turned away from the camera, facing Mr. Meth.

Derek zoomed back in again, focusing on the driver.

I squinted at the screen, watching the driver glance around, looking up and down the street, checking if he was alone. At one point his gaze went straight at Derek's car. It was just a flash, but his face was immediately recognizable to anyone who watched the news.

Mayor Sean Brumhill.

His term had ended last year, but at the time this video was shot he'd been known for his tough fight against crime, especially drugs. Which raised my radar as the meth head stepped forward and opened Brumhill's passenger side door, getting into the car. He pulled something from his jacket pocket. A thick wad of cash. He handed it to Brumhill, who flipped through the stack, and nodded. Then he ducked out of the car, and Brumhill sped away.

The video stopped.

I sat back, my mind running through what I just watched. A payoff. For what, I wasn't sure, but I knew it was nothing good. A bribe? A reward for "looking the other way"? No matter what the explanation, Derek had shot video damning enough that it would have not only ended the Mayor's term early, but possibly his entire career.

This was huge.

This was beyond huge.

This was a reason to want the videographer dead.

# CHAPTER TWELVE

———

I stepped into the agency the next morning and spotted a man in the conference room. My next prospective client. I stopped at Maya's desk before greeting him.

She handed me a short stack of messages, then gestured to the conference room behind her. "That is Mr. Fleming."

"Has he been waiting long?" I checked my watch. The appointment wasn't for another ten minutes, but suspecting spouses were notoriously anxious.

"Not even long enough to sip the coffee I brought him." She winked and handed me his file. "He checks out."

"Thanks." I started to turn away and stopped. "How'd things go with your mother after I left?"

Maya nodded. "Surprisingly okay. Thanks for all the glowing reviews."

"Glad to help," I told her. Not that I thought I'd fixed all of her issues with Mom, but at least she knew how her daughter was valued at work. It was a start.

"She's actually meeting me for lunch today," Maya said.

"Wow, two days in a row? You're brave," I joked.

She grinned. "Yeah, well, Mom said after yesterday she wanted to see where I worked. I figured it wasn't a bad idea."

"Well have fun." I paused. "And take a long lunch if you want," I called over my shoulder as I tossed my things into my office then headed to the conference room.

Caleigh met me along the way and fell into step. "Need a second pair of ears?"

"Always." Like myself, Caleigh had an appreciation for expensive suits, and Mr. Fleming, I noticed, wore a navy Armani. We had a strict no-dating-the-clients policy, but once the case was finished, the girls could do as they wanted. And considering the end of the case usually meant divorce court, this business was the perfect place to meet people. Unfortunately, ninety-nine percent of our clients were women, so a male client was like ice cream in July.

I pushed open the door, and Mr. Fleming rose, extending his hand. His grip was firm and warm. Soft, callous-free fingers suggested he worked in an office. I hadn't yet taken the time to peruse the background information Maya had provided me, but I knew she'd thoroughly vetted him.

"I'm Jamie Bond, and this is my colleague, Caleigh Presley."

"Second cousin once removed to Elvis," she said in a thicker than normal drawl.

He offered a polite smile, nodded at each of us. Then Mr. Fleming and I took our seats while Caleigh strutted to the beverage cart in the corner and poured herself a glass of water. She bent over, her dress clinging to her backside seductively. I had to admit, if I was a man, I'd be curious what other seductions she had up her…skirt.

"How did you hear of us, Mr. Fleming?"

"Please call me Craig. Mrs. Martin recommended you. We play tennis together."

"How may we help you?"

"I think my spouse is cheating." He twirled his wedding band around his finger.

Caleigh took the seat beside him and leaned forward ever so slightly, giving him full view of her cleavage. "That's horrible."

I expected her to start purring at any moment. While Caleigh usually went for the muscle-bound guys in fitted tanks and pants so tight she knew exactly what she was getting into, she must have caught the scent of money coming from Craig as well as I did. Craig was an attractive man for late thirties, a light dusting of gray at his temples, which blended well into his short, sandy brown hair. Clear blue eyes and a firm jaw. He had a slim, but not overly gym-dedicated physique.

"What gives you reason to believe infidelity?" I asked.

Craig cleared his throat, the words obviously hard to say. "Whispered phone conversations, later than usual nights at work."

The typical reasons. I scribbled notes onto a pad of paper.

"Do you have any idea with whom, or where they get together? Any suspicious credit charges or receipts?"

He reached into his pocket and pulled out a folded napkin. "I found this in the laundry."

A husband who did laundry? What kind of fool would cheat on that?

I took the napkin and unfolded it, expecting to see a scrawled phone number or other come-on. Instead, I received a different kind of surprise. The name of the bar was Cock Tails, with a martini glass in the center, separating the innocuous word into something much more. I'd never been there but had heard of the place in passing. A giggle sat in my throat, ready to erupt.

I flipped open the file and scanned the top page.

Client: Craig Fleming, 39, Human Resources' manager at United Life. An insurance company.

Spouse: Phillip Marchand, 28, rising actor-slash-server

I looked up and smiled. "So, this isn't a place you and Phillip normally visit?"

Caleigh's eyes widened. It took a second, but then the information sank in, and she pulled up the collar of her top while leaning back into her seat. Poor Caleigh.

"Not now, no. It's where Phillip and I met four years ago. He was one of the bartenders." Craig sniffled.

I pushed a box of tissues toward him.

He took one out but just held it. "We hit it off immediately. None of those games people play. He was honest and upfront. He said he was looking for something meaningful. I didn't trust it at first. He was so young. But we started dating, and soon I realized he was serious. We've been together ever since. We got married six months ago."

Maybe making it legal had tightened an invisible noose around Phillip's neck. This wouldn't be the first time a guy did something stupid when fear of commitment took over.

"And when did this suspicious behavior begin?"

"Last month."

"Have you done any investigating of your own?"

Caleigh asked.

It was usually the first step wives took. Trail the husband, see where he went. Sometimes their mates were too stupid to be careful, and the wife never had to call us. Just knock on a motel room door with a cell phone camera.

Craig nodded. "Yes. A couple of times I waited outside the restaurant where he works, but both times he just stopped for gas or a candy bar. He has a severe sweet tooth." A smile nudged the corners of his mouth.

"But you never followed him there?" I pointed to the napkin.

He shook his head. "No. I only found that this morning." His voice cracked.

Caleigh's brows puckered. She placed one hand on his wrist, and patted his back with the other. Seductress one moment and mother the next.

I jotted down more details, giving Craig time to collect himself. Then I looked up and continued. "When are his nights off? When is he likely to head to this bar?"

"Tonight and Monday nights. He has those days off when he's not going to auditions."

"Okay, we're going to find out what's going on. We'll follow Phillip and learn his behaviors. If he's cheating, we'll know. But before we begin, I have to ask, are you certain you want to know?"

It was a ridiculous question. How could someone say no, walk out of here, and live with herself, or in this case, himself? But as crazy as it sounded, it had happened once. A young wife, so deeply in love that the idea of being without her husband was worse than putting up his infidelities. Sam and I had been sitting outside a fancy restaurant, watching the husband and his assistant eating steak and lobster, while we were munching on Cheetos and coffee, when the wife called my cell and fired us. She couldn't handle it and would just believe her husband's lies. Ever since then, I asked.

Craig sat straight and stared into my eyes. He didn't blink or look away for a second. "Yes. I have to know."

I nodded my acceptance. "Did you bring a photo of Phillip?"

"Yes." He reached into a brown leather messenger bag on the floor by his chair and pulled out a five-by-seven photo of him and Phillip. On their wedding day.

I thanked Craig, assured him once again that we'd get to the truth, then let Caleigh show him out to the lobby while I studied the photograph.

Both men wore white suits and shirts. Both beamed into the camera, standing cheek-to-cheek. And both held one another's hand, high, in front of their chests, showing off a single gold band on each ring finger. They looked like the perfect ornament for the top of a cake. At first, all I saw was how deliriously happy they looked. Then I noticed their slight differences. Phillip was dark to where Craig was light—hair, skin-tone, eyes. Craig was a couple of inches shorter. And while Phillip's skin was so smooth that it looked like he lived in a moisturized bubble, never going out into the smog-filled world, Craig's infectious smile displayed tiny lines at the corners of his eyes and mouth.

My chest tugged. I hoped this time the client would be wrong. But what else was young, beautiful Phillip doing at Cock Tails?

Unfortunately, it was clear that to find that out, my girls were going to be useless. They had zero chance of playing the enticing eye candy.

I grabbed my cell, scrolling through my contacts until I saw his name, and dialed. Two rings in, Danny picked up.

"What time is it?" he croaked.

I ignored what I hoped was a rhetorical question. "Hey, remember last night how you said two heads are better than one?"

"Sure," he said, clearing the sleep from his voice.

"Well, I need your help."

"You got it. What's up?"

"That new client I told you about. We're tailing the spouse tonight at a club."

"Sounds fun," he responded, and I could hear the sounds of shuffling accompanied by his coffee maker hissing to life. "What kind of pictures you need? Because I have this new camera I've been wanting to try out. Fits onto a pair of sunglasses, the sucker is so small."

"Actually, I need you to play decoy this time." I hoped he didn't hear the hitch in my voice. Danny was as straight as a guy got. I had to word my request very carefully.

"Oh, really?" His voice went up an interested notch. "So your client is the husband this time."

I nodded slowly. "Yes, his name is Craig."

"And he thinks his wife is cheating? Did he show you pictures? Is she hot?"

I suppressed a grin. Was it wrong that a part of me was kind of enjoying stringing Danny along? "Yes, his spouse is very attractive. Eleven years younger than Craig."

I could practically hear Danny's smile through the line. "Well then I'm happy to put my skills to good use for you. When do you need me?"

"Nine-ish?"

He paused. "What do you say we meet at eight for a light dinner first?"

I bit the inside of my cheek. "I'm kind of busy today," I answered, thinking just as much about how I *wanted* to follow up on the video I'd seen last night as how much I *didn't* want to know what this mysterious "something" Danny wanted to talk to me about might be. The truth was, Danny and I hung out, we met up, we palled around. We didn't really talk. And I wasn't sure I wanted to know why we were starting now.

"Busy, huh?"

"Let's uh, just meet here at the office. That way we can set up the cameras and wire the girls before we hit the club."

"Caleigh and Sam going, too?"

"Yes. It's all hands on deck for this one."

I thought I detected the slightest bit of disappointment in Danny's pause, but it was covered so quickly maybe I imagined it. "Anything else I should know?" he asked.

If I told Danny the truth now, that gave him almost ten hours to come up with an excuse to back out. Better to blindside him and beg once we got there. "Nope. See you at nine."

\* \* \*

As soon as I got off the phone with Danny, I barricaded myself in my office and booted up my computer, scouring the internet for any info on Mayor Brumhill. While I tried to keep up with the big news stories, I had to admit that I was not a news devotee. There was too much depressing stuff on the news, ninety percent of it things I couldn't do anything about anyway. I read through half a dozen articles about the mayor from around the time Bernstein was shot. Balancing the city budget, dedicating a new library, cutting funds for parks, but allocating more to police efforts. None shed any light on why the mayor would be taking wads of cash from meth heads. Clearly whatever the mayor had been into, the media had not been privy to. It wouldn't be a stretch to imagine that Derek had been the only one to witness it. I didn't even want to speculate why Derek had kept it in a drawer under this spare bunk instead of bringing it to the attention of the DA's office like a good, law-abiding citizen. I didn't want to deal with the answer to that question yet.

Once I got tired of reading about the mayor's sparkling record, I switched gears, focusing on the guy I'd seen paying him off. I had very little to go on, so I started with the jacket he'd been wearing. If he was in a gang, it was possible the lion was some sort of insignia.

After an hour of pouring over gang activity websites, I gave up. If there was some way to identify this guy, it was beyond my skills. I looked down at my watch. I had half an hour before I had to meet Aiden.

I grabbed my purse and walked into the lobby to find Charley hovering over Maya's desk as her daughter shut down her computer screen. The older woman wore another yellow sundress, but she'd added a white linen jacket over it today. "Hello, Jamie, so nice to see you again." She took my hand and squeezed it.

"You, too," I told her.

"Well, we're headed to lunch," Maya said. "Do you need anything before we go?"

"No, have a great time."

Charley hesitated, as if she wanted to say something. But she didn't. Instead she just smiled my way as she walked out with her daughter.

I followed their lead, hopping into my Roadster and heading toward the 2.

I stepped into Cafe Monroe precisely at noon. The rush of air conditioning was a welcome respite from the heat outside already climbing into the triple digits. The place was an indoor-slash-outdoor cafe that served breakfast and lunch, and was just blocks from the studios. Which meant that on a day like today, the indoor section was packed. I gave the hostess Aiden's name and followed her past the tables of boisterous chatter. I smiled with relief when I noticed he was seated by the French doors that led to an outside patio, but firmly on the side of the blessed forced air. A large potted palm sat opposite, on the patio, blocking the sunlight some, so instead of it flooding the round, mosaic-glassed tabletop, it formed small peaks of light, making the intricate design sparkle.

Aiden stood as I approached, and he held my seat out for me. His smile was warm, genuine, and made my stomach curl in a not unpleasant way.

"Hey, beautiful," he said, giving me a peck on the cheek.

"Hey, yourself," I answered. Aiden was in his court attire—Brooks Brothers suit, shiny wing-tips, perfectly knotted tie and clean shaven cheeks. He looked like an ad for *GQ*, and he smelled even better, his subtle aftershave wafting across the table toward me.

A server arrived, and we quickly ordered a pair of iced teas. I chose the avocado shrimp wrap with baby spinach, tomato, a spicy cumin dressing, and crumbled feta cheese. Aiden ordered a turkey sandwich with a side of fries. As soon as the server left, Aiden turned his attention on me. "How's your morning been?"

I nodded. "Good. Uneventful. How was court?"

His expression lost some of its luster. "I'll be resting my case right after lunch. My last witness is this afternoon. Then it's the defense's turn."

That was fast. But as Aiden had mentioned, it was an open and shut case. As long as the evidence was damning enough, I suppose he didn't need a mountain of it. "Who's your last witness?" I asked.

He hesitated, as usual. It was our normal way of

communicating. I'd ask a question and hold my breath, wondering if he'd answer or put up that ADA wall. It was getting to the point where I was no longer holding my breath and waiting. He either answered or didn't, and in the meantime, I studied his firm jaw and the liquid blue of his eyes.

"Jillian. Brady's girlfriend."

Whoa, that was surprising. "You think she has knowledge of Bernstein's death?"

Unfortunately, he didn't get a chance to respond as our food arrived, and we took a moment to stare at our plates. My wrap was enormous, and I cut it in half. Aiden's sandwich was the same, but I watched him toy with the idea of which half to lift first. It seemed no matter what choice he made, it was going to fall apart, and he'd end up using a fork. He stuffed a napkin into his collar and created a paper bib. He took a bite and surprisingly, it all held together.

I did the same and spent the next minute celebrating the joy that exploded in my mouth. If I'd been alone, I would've done a happy dance in my chair and probably made some orgasmic moans.

"So, Jillian. You think she can add something about Bernstein's death?" I asked again.

Aiden shook his head. "I don't think she has details to the murder, no. But she's a witness to Brady's character. She's lived with him for years. And they aren't married. There's no spousal privilege."

In the immortal words of Beyoncé, he should've put a ring on it. "So what do you think she'll say?" I asked, wondering just how much trash-talk he could get out of her. I had the feeling that Jillian wasn't altogether happy with her man, but I wasn't sure she was ready to hang him out to dry either.

Aiden gave me a tight smile. "Police have been to Jillian's place a couple of times on domestic battery. She's never pressed charges, but I'm hoping to establish a history of anger management issues."

My heart broke for Jillian. She deserved so much better. Part of me hoped the trial was the kick in the pants she needed to finally move on.

We chewed for a few minutes in silence. The chatter

around us changed as tables cleared and new customers arrived. When I looked up, I found Aiden staring at me.

"What?"

He grinned and shook his head. "Nothing. You just look like you're really enjoying that sandwich."

"It's the best. Wanna taste?"

He shook his head. "I'll pass. I prefer a little meat in my meal. And grease," he said, gesturing to his French fries. Which, by the way, smelled like heaven. It was all I could do to keep myself from stealing one off of his plate.

He must have seen the moral dilemma in my eyes, as he held up one crispy, delicious looking fry. "Want one?"

I pursed my lips together and shook my head. "No thanks. I've got to fit into a slinky cocktail dress tonight."

He raised an eyebrow my way.

"A case," I explained. "We're counting on a cheating spouse to make an appearance at his favorite meat market."

"It's a good thing I'm not the jealous type," he told me, a teasing grin playing at the corner of his mouth."

I shot him an answering one. "Well, you don't have anything to worry about on this one. It's a gay club."

Aiden laughed out loud, an explosive sound that made my stomach do that warm, curling thing again. Only this time it was tempered with a little guilt. While the sandwich was awesome, I had ulterior motives for meeting him for lunch today.

"Hey, what do you know about Mayor Brumhill?" I asked, doing my best nonchalance act.

He shrugged. "Ex-mayor. Well respected. I can't say I've worked with him myself." Which wasn't surprising, since Aiden had only moved to California and taken over as ADA a few months ago.

"Have you heard anything that might raise a red flag about him? Any rumors or sour grapes from his former cabinet?" I was taking a huge gamble asking Aiden. My nosing around about a politician would raise the hairs on the back of his neck for sure.

He took a moment, looked off outside, then returned to our conversation. "I met him at a fundraiser last month. Charming guy. Soft, doughy hands with a weak handshake."

I grinned. "Does that mean something?"

"Not necessarily. My daddy always said that a man's handshake showed his character."

"Your daddy? That sounds Texan. I thought you were from Kansas City."

"I am. My mother's hometown. But my father was born in Fort Worth and raised in Dallas, thirty minutes up the road. Mom went to college there. She wanted to live someplace warm that didn't get snow. They met and fell in love." He paused. "Then she experienced her first southern summer and wanted to return to the snow."

We shared a laughed before he went on.

"He followed her and proposed. He said he'd endure the Arctic if it meant being by her side. But we'd go to Dallas a couple of times a year to visit his family."

How sweet and romantic. Something that seemed a million miles away from real life here in the cheating metropolis. I let my mind wander over the image of little Aiden eating barbeque with his southern cousins, both sides giggling at the accents. Of Aiden between his proud, happy parents—a traditional family. "They're both still alive?"

"Yes."

A wave of envy washed over me, but I quickly rode it out. I was used to others talking about their parents and how they needed to call or were going over for dinner on the weekend. It wasn't shocking. But every once in a while, it rattled me, and memories of Mom's death would flood my body. "That's great."

He cupped my hand, knowing my past. I wasn't the only one who'd experienced death, though. Aiden got a faraway look in his eyes, and I assumed he was remembering his wife. I definitely didn't want to end our lunch date on that much of a sour note.

"So, Brumhill."

Aiden nodded, pulling his hands back to his meal. "Right. I honestly can't say I've heard any rumors about him. Why?"

I shrugged. I'd been ready for that question. "His name came up in a routine investigation. A friend of a friend kind of thing."

He didn't push. I couldn't tell if he believed me or not, but if I didn't get to know the ins and outs of his prosecutor work, then he didn't need insight into mine either. It was only fair, and justice was all about fairness, right? That's why the blindfolded woman held a scale.

"So, that slinky dress?" Aiden said, switching gears. "Does it have plans for after you catch your cheater tonight?"

I felt a flirty smile snake across my face. "What did you have in mind?"

A slow grin showed two rows of perfectly straight white teeth. "You. Me. A night out." He paused. "Or maybe even a night in."

There went that warmth again, spreading to places completely inappropriate to discuss in a crowded cafe. I smiled big. "I'm all yours."

# CHAPTER THIRTEEN

———

Caleigh, Sam, and I were seated in the lobby of the agency when Danny came in. He wore a light blue T-shirt that highlighted the blue flecks in his eyes today with a pair of pressed, light gray pants, jacket, and matching loafers. Very old *Miami Vice*, but somehow it looked modern and cool on him. He'd gelled his hair, making him look polished and playful all at the same time. He looked every bit the guy out for a good time tonight.

"Nice outfit," I commented truthfully.

Danny let his eyes roam my little black dress. Emphasis on the *little* part. "Ditto."

"I try," I said, shrugging the comment off, even though my ego enjoyed it just the teeniest bit.

Danny set up my laptop with the feed from our hidden cameras, and then we left, Danny and me in my car, Sam and Caleigh following behind. It wasn't until we were sitting in traffic on the 101 that Danny finally asked the dreaded question.

"So, where are we headed?"

"A club," I hedged.

"Which one?"

"It's called Cock Tails," I told him, watching his reaction out of the corner of my eye.

He frowned and rubbed the back of his neck. "I don't think I've been there. Cocktails?"

I cleared my throat. "It's actually cock…tails," I told him, pausing the appropriate amount of time between the two words to infuse them with meaning.

Danny shot me a look. "Jamie, what kind of club is this?"

"It might be just a little bit…gay."

"Sonofa—" Danny shook his head, the look on his face telling me that if we hadn't been in the middle of the freeway, he totally would have bolted. "No way. Oh, no. There's no way I'm hitting on a dude!"

"Come on, Danny, you know I can't do it."

"And just when were you planning on springing this little detail on me?" he asked.

I shrugged. "I thought you'd figure it out about the time we got there."

He shot me a death look. "That's low, Bond. Really low."

"Look, I'm sorry I didn't tell you, but you never would have gotten into the car with me if you'd known."

"Damn straight."

"See?" I said. Which did nothing to strengthen my case.

"I can't do this," he muttered. "I don't know how to hit on guys."

"It can't be that different than girls, and you're an expert there."

"Oh, it's different," he said, still shaking his head. "Trust me."

"Look, it's one night. Maybe two. Just long enough for you to sweet talk him into grabbing your ass."

His eyes flew wide, and if I didn't reel him in immediately, I knew I'd lose him altogether.

"Please, Danny. I need you. I'm not asking for anything you can't do. It's just acting. It's not real. No one is going to truly believe you're gay." I paused. "Except our mark."

Danny shook his head, eyes staring out the window.

"Please," I pleaded again as I pulled off the freeway, taking the 2 toward West Hollywood. "For me?"

"Do I have a choice?" he huffed.

Which I took as his way of conceding. We pulled up to Cock Tails, hitting the valet line right behind Sam and Caleigh. I handed over the keys, and Danny and I got out. Me watching him so he didn't take off, him pouting like a two-year-old.

"Here." I showed him Craig and Phillip's wedding photo. "This is our target. The dark-haired one."

He eyed it suspiciously, like it would bite him in the

nose if he stared for too long. "Nice hair."

"See? You have something in common already." I couldn't hide the desperation in my tone.

He must've noticed it because he took the photo, brought it close to his face, then handed it back. "Fine. Let's do this." He paused. "But you owe me now, Bond," he said stabbing a finger my way.

I nodded in agreement. "Totally."

Sam and Caleigh, who had been bravely pun and comment-free until this point, let out deep breaths. They must've felt relieved, too. Caleigh did her bounce-on-her-toes routine, and Danny marched ahead of us.

"This is going to be fun," Sam whispered. I couldn't tell if she meant it or was being sarcastic.

We allowed Danny to go in first and gave him a couple of minutes to scope out the place. Normally, I would've preferred if we had settled in first, but I didn't like the idea of leaving Danny outside alone. I wasn't 100% convinced he wouldn't still bolt if given the chance.

As we fought through the crowd, I did a quick perusal of the layout. It wasn't a big place, half a dozen tables, a large area for dancing by the DJ station, and a chrome bar that ran the length of one wall. Danny sat at the bar, looking distinctly uncomfortable. The place was packed with customers, all men except for us, though most were on the dance floor, leaving a scant few at the tables.

One of the guys sitting was a young Brad Pitt lookalike, from his Thelma and Louise days. He sat alone, nursing a dark stout and flirting with a server. Two others wore white Polo shirts, shorts, socks, and matching sneakers, and looked like they came straight from the tennis courts or golf course. The stark white against their tanned skin almost made them glow. They laughed and chatted and sipped what looked like mai tais.

I approached the bar, while Caleigh went into the bathroom and Sam settled at the other end of the bar. The bartender took my order then Sam's, while we pretended we didn't know one another. I took my martini to a table in the corner, Sam stayed at the bar, and Caleigh returned, ordering herself a Cosmopolitan. Once she received it, she sat at a table beside the couple. We were in view of Danny, but if the place grew more crowded, we'd have to get closer. I took a deep breath and sipped my drink. Perfect.

"That was the first time a bartender hasn't flirted with me," Caleigh whispered into her mic, her sultry voice caressing my ear.

Sam smiled. Danny remained motionless.

I lifted my collar and pushed the microphone disguised as a button. "You okay, Danny?"

He nodded then cleared his throat, nearly blowing out my eardrum. "Just parched." He tilted his beer to his lips and guzzled.

Uh-oh, we needed to make sure he didn't get drunk and ruin our cover.

I scanned the crowd for our mark, hoping to make this a quick mission. While the dance area held a healthy number of patrons, I spotted Phillip easily. Even among L.A.'s beautiful people, his good looks stood out. And in person, he was even more stunning than his photograph. No wonder Craig was worried.

Sam must have followed my gaze. "Show time," she mumbled.

Danny turned, spotted Philip, then mumbled, "I'm not dancing with him," as he downed the rest of his beer.

I bit my lip. "Fine. He'll need a drink sooner or later. Just sit tight."

Danny nodded, signaling the bartender for another. Luckily, it was sooner rather than later when Phillip detangled himself from the crowd and hit the bar, planting himself on the stool directly to Danny's right. Excellent.

"Usual?" I heard the bartender ask him through Danny's mic.

Phillip nodded, and the bartender made him a whiskey sour. He was definitely a regular. I watched Phillip's eyes scan the other patrons, though if he was looking for someone in particular or just looking, I couldn't tell.

Danny cleared his throat, then turned to Philip. "Hey," he said.

I rolled my eyes. "'Hey?' I know you've got better pick-up lines than that, Danny."

He ignored me, instead addressing Philip again. "How's your day been?"

If Philip was interested, he knew how to play cool. "Long. You?"

Danny nodded. "Same here. Photo shoot fell through yesterday, and I don't get paid when the model gets sent home for being young and unprofessional." He took another long drink, finishing the damn thing, and ordered another. I started keeping a mental tally.

"You're a photographer?" Philip asked.

That was always a good conversation starter.

"Yeah." Danny's hand trembled as he raised the third bottle to his mouth.

"Slow down. You don't want to get drunk," I whispered into my cleavage.

"You said model, as in fashion or…"

Danny put the bottle down. "Top cover. Ever hear of Echo St. Pierre?"

"No, I don't follow the fashion scene. But that means you're probably expensive, right?"

"It depends. Why? Are you looking to have pictures done?"

Phillip turned his body toward Danny, sitting on the stool sideways. "I'm an actor. Done a few commercials, but I really want to break into film. A new portfolio would help, but I'm not sure I can afford it. I'm on a budget right now. Trying to save up."

Sam shifted on her stool. "Saving up to leave hubby?" she mumbled.

"Buying a new car?" Danny asked.

"No, nothing like that. Just for my future. I'm Phillip." He held out his hand.

Danny hesitated but then extended his. "Danny."

He rubbed the back of his neck then turned toward Phillip. Their knees touched. Danny glanced down at the connection, but there was no way to move unless he wanted to sit with one of his legs between Phillip's, or vice versa. He stayed put. "This is my first time here. What's it like?"

Phillip glanced around the club, again as if looking for someone. "It's friendly. You won't get hassled or hit on, unless you want to." He winked.

Danny chuckled, but his wide-eyed stare suggested terror.

Caleigh giggled. Sam snorted. Danny shot me an evil glare, and I bit my bottom lip.

"So, not the place a guy goes who's looking to score?" Danny asked. I was proud of him. Despite his discomfort, the suggestive tone in his voice was unmistakable.

Phillip didn't respond at first. He toyed with the napkin beside his glass "I don't do drugs."

"No, I didn't mean…" He started to place a hand on Philip's knee, but snatched it back before it made contact, rubbing the back of his neck again instead. "I—uh, so how about the Lakers? Do you follow basketball?"

"Nah, it's not really my sport."

It wasn't Danny's either.

This was pathetic. I whispered, "Get on with it. Open up. Loosen up. Be friendly. Pry."

A few more patrons moved toward the bar, and I repositioned myself just as Phillip's cell chimed. I watched him pull it from his pocket, check the readout, then frown.

"Everything okay?" Danny asked.

"Yeah, sure." Philip shoved the cell back into his jeans. "Just…the guy I was meeting tonight just cancelled on me."

"Sucks to be stood up," Danny said.

Philip gave him a small smile. "It's something like that."

"So you're married?" Danny pointed to Phillip's left hand. "Was your husband meeting you?"

"No. He doesn't know I'm here."

Bingo. I felt myself leaning in.

"Oh? Do tell," Danny prompted.

"It's…nothing."

"He's not going to spill to a stranger," Caleigh whispered.

Danny drummed his fingers on the top of the bar. "So, what hobbies are you into?"

God, this was painful to listen to. It sounded like a bad

night of speed dating.

"Not much. Auditions take up a big chunk of my time."

"Yeah, I hear ya. I date. A lot."

Phillip chuckled. "You have a great body. You must have the guys all over you."

Danny's complexion warmed to a rosy pink. He cleared his throat. "I guess. Movies. I like movies. *Indiana Jones*, *The Mummy*, action and adventure stuff."

"The classics. How about *Inception* and *Mission Impossible*?"

"Not a huge fan of Tom Cruise, but Matt Damon…"

"Hot, right?"

And they were off. They spent the next half-hour talking about movies and ended up sounding more like two old friends than possible hook ups.

Around eleven, Phillip glanced at his watch and threw some money on the bar. "I have to get going. This has been fun."

Danny looked panicked. "Yeah, I had a great time. Do you have to leave now? It's still early."

"Not for me. Early audition." He slid off the stool and cupped Danny's shoulder. "We should hang out again some time."

Yes!

Danny fumbled in his pocket and pulled out a business card. "Here. Call me. Or I could call you."

"Sure." Phillip put the card into his back pocket then asked the bartender for a pen. He grabbed Danny's hand, wrote on his palm, like a girl in junior high, and left.

Caleigh sighed loudly. "I bet he'll never wash that hand again."

\* \* \*

After Philip left, I avoided eye contact with Danny and drove him home in silence. I wasn't sure if he was still pissed at my deception or embarrassed at having successfully gotten a guy's number, but either way he wasn't in a speaking-to-me mood. I figured it was best to let him have his space, filling the ride with the radio instead. As soon as I dropped him at his building, I texted Aiden.

*I'm free now. Meet at my place?*

Two minutes later a response lit up my screen.

*Be there in 20 min.*

Which gave me just long enough to get home and freshen up. I pulled into traffic and made it back to my apartment in record time. I chilled a bottle of wine, threw on a little mood music, and changed from the industrial Spanx that had held my Glock in place to a pair of lacy itty-bitty bikini panties, and dabbed on a little perfume. I was just reapplying my lipstick when I heard Aiden's shave-and-a-hair-cut knock at the front door, sending a little shiver of anticipation up my spine.

I opened the door and immediately felt glad I'd gone with the itty-bitties. Aiden was dressed in a pair of slacks, a button-down shirt, open at the collar, and he held one red rose in his hands. It took all I had not to jump him right there in my doorway.

"Hey," I said.

He grinned. "Hey yourself, beautiful."

"The rose is a nice touch," I said, gesturing to the flower.

Aiden shrugged. "It never hurts to arrive with a little romance in hand."

I took it from him, and he leaned in, giving me a light kiss on the cheek. He smelled like soap and aftershave. I inhaled deeply. Oh, this was going to be a good night.

"Nice music," Aiden commented as he came into the room. "Nora Jones?"

"Uh-huh," I answered. "I figure it never hurts to have a little romance in the air." I gave him a wink.

Aiden laughed, a deep, rich thing. Then he lightly grabbed my hand and pulled me toward him. "I guess we're on the same page, then."

I swallowed, my heart hammering in my chest. "I think so," I said, my voice coming out way more breathless than I'd meant it to.

Though it didn't seem to faze Aiden. He just gave me one of his lady-killer smiles, all big blue eyes and genuine affection, then leaned in, his lips softly covering mine.

I think I sighed, my knees giving out just a little as his

arms wound around my middle. I wrapped my own around his neck, my hands going to his hair. It was soft and a little wet from the shower still. I held onto it for dear life as Aiden kissed me. I was instant putty. His lips were warm and insistent, kissing me like he meant it. I don't know how long we got lost in each other like that, but when we came up for air, Aiden's hair was a wreck and I was panting like a cat in heat.

His eyes cut to my bedroom, in a silent question.

I was just about to answer along the lines of, "Hell, yes," when my phone went off from my purse.

I froze, thought a few bad words, then quickly reached into my clutch and checked the readout. Private number. I hit the button to send it to voicemail. Let them leave a message.

"You need to take that?" Aiden asked. I was pleased to note that his voice sounded as breathless as mine had been a few minutes ago.

I shook my head. "I'm sure it's nothing. It can wait."

Aiden grinned, took a step toward me.

Then my phone rang again.

Sonofa-

"It's okay," Aiden chuckled. "Go ahead and see what they want. I can wait."

I shot him a grateful look before stabbing the on button. I swear to God if this was a telemarketer…

"What?" I barked.

"Jamie?" came a tentative voice. "Is this you? I don't know if I dialed the right number. I'm so frazzled, and they're staring at me as if I stole the Queen's jewels."

I glanced at the clock above my dining table. It was past midnight. "Who is this?"

"Oh, sorry, dear. This is Charley. Maya's mom?"

My pulse quickened. Why was she calling me so late? "Charley, what's wrong? Is Maya okay? Are you okay?"

"Yes, we're fine. Well, I guess she is. She's home. I…well, I need your help. I didn't want to call and worry her, and you're the only other person I thought of when they allowed me to use the phone."

A sinking feeling hit my stomach like a cement brick. "Charley, where are you?"

"I've been arrested."

# CHAPTER FOURTEEN

———

I followed the young, pimply cop down the narrow corridor of cells, to the last one. Why did they always file prisoners in the last one first? It was as if they wanted to torture the person just a bit more by parading them in front of the cells, especially the innocent little old ladies.

Charley and Ruth were huddled on a bench and whispering. Charley looked up, saw me, and smiled. She rushed to the bars and grabbed my hands through them. "I knew you'd help."

"How could I not?" I glanced to Pimply. Or Hodkins, according to his name tag. "Thanks."

He nodded. "I can only give you ten minutes tops."

"I understand."

He nodded again and walked back up front to his desk. Visiting hours were long over, and I wasn't family or an attorney, but Pim…Hodkins snuck me in. It was partly due to his feeling bad when he locked me up a few months ago—in this exact cell, I might add—and partly because I shamelessly flirted.

"Are you going to bust us out?" Charley asked, eyes wide with excitement.

Did she think I hid a metal nail file in my shoe?

"Maya is talking with Ruth's neighbor, trying to get the charges dropped. What happened?"

Ruth dropped her head into her hands and moaned.

Charley squeezed my fingers. Her pained expression matched the cramp she was causing in my pinky. "I didn't want Maya involved."

"She has to be. She's your daughter, and when the courts let you out on bail, it's better if family's there."

"Very well. It's all a big misunderstanding anyway."

Ruth shook her head. "Are you crazy? We broke into their house. Just because I know the alarm code doesn't make it legal."

Charley and I both shushed her in unison. You never admitted guilt inside the police station.

Ruth lowered her voice until I could barely make out her words. "Well, it's true. I should've just left it alone, ignored it. I'd been doing that for months now anyway. Why did I have to listen to you and try to get proof?"

She folded her arms across her chest and turned her body toward the back wall, away from us, like a pouting child.

"What is she talking about?" I asked.

Charley rolled her eyes. "Ruth believes her husband, Frank, is cheating on her with her neighbor, Belle."

It all suddenly made sense. Charley's sudden interest in Maya's job, her boss, all the PI questions at lunch.

"Where's Abigail?" I asked.

"She chickened out at the last minute."

Smart woman.

"So tell me, what happened?"

Ruth shot Charley a glare.

Charley hesitated. "You're not a lawyer, dear."

She was right. Anything they told me I'd be sworn to divulge. I couldn't do that to them. "Okay, then tell me why Ruth thinks Frank is cheating."

Charley glanced to her friend. When Ruth didn't respond in any way, Charley turned to me full on and talked at rapid speed. "Last month, Frank went over to Belle's to fix her toilet. The poor, delicate creature didn't know how to use a plunger. Can you believe that? She's been widowed for five years, and that was her first clogged john? I don't think so. Anyway, Frank was gone a little too long, and when he returned, he smelled of wine. I guess Belle insisted he share a nightcap with her. The following week it was a leak in her kitchen sink, then a bathtub that needed caulking, and her refrigerator went out. Could he help her with her meat? I mean, really?"

I bit my lower lip to refrain from giggling. Charley was an enthusiastic storyteller.

"Last night, Ruth went over to see what was really going

on. She'd been mildly suspicious at this point."

"Only because you and Abigail insisted he was cheating." Ruth's voice was tight and full of emotion. Poor woman. She obviously hadn't wanted to believe it until her friends stepped in and convinced her to stare at reality.

"A man can only hold out for so long. And we were right, no?" Charley cringed after her words. "I'm sorry. I don't need to be right. I'm just looking out for you."

Ruth glanced over, her eyes brimming with unshed tears.

Charley went to the bench, sat by her friend, and wrapped her arms around her. She leaned her chin on Ruth's shoulder and repeated, "It's going to be okay."

My chest tightened at the sincere exchange. These two were great friends. I didn't have anyone like that in my life. Danny was a true friend, sure, but it wasn't the same. Sam and Caleigh. I trusted them with my life, but not necessarily the details of my *personal* life. I never thought to turn to one of them for advice. They were my girls. But I hadn't confided in any of them about my current side case about who shot Derek.

After a moment, Ruth patted Charley's arm. Charley released her and rejoined me. "Last night Ruth went next door and heard them laughing and chatting through the open front door. They were seated on the living room couch, facing one another, a little too close. They were drinking, and Frank had his arm draped over the back of the sofa. Belle was running her fingers up and down his arm. Ruth knocked on the door and Frank jumped, spilling his wine. She tried entering, but the screen was locked. When they came to the door, Frank looked guilty. And Belle looked…"

"Gleeful," Ruth said.

I sighed. "Did you ask him?"

"Yes. He denied it."

"And tonight was about getting proof?"

Charley nodded. "What is Maya doing?"

"The police told us that Ruth's neighbor, Mrs. McGuffey, was pressing charges for breaking and entering. She went to talk with her, to get her to drop them."

"Belle will never agree to it," Ruth said. "She's thrilled I'm in here and Frank is home alone."

"What happens if Belle refuses?" Charley asked.

"You'll go to arraignment in the morning. You're lucky it's not the weekend. And the judge will probably release you on bail. You'll both need lawyers."

Ruth's shoulders began to tremble. Her cry was silent.

"It will be okay. You'll probably just get some probation. It's your first offense. Right?"

Charley nodded. "Yes, but I don't think she's as worried about jail time as she is about leaving Frank alone."

"So you did get proof?"

"No. The police arrived before we were able to."

"Isn't it possible he's not cheating?"

Charley gave me an "are you dumb" stare.

"Sometimes looks can be deceiving. Just because Belle sounds like a home-wrecking tramp doesn't mean Frank's taken her up on it. Some men just like their ego stroked, but they don't stray." Some. A few. I hid my skepticism. Ruth needed to be stroked too.

She stood on wobbly legs and walked over to us. "That's possible?"

"Anything is possible. Would you like me to look into it?"

Charley and Ruth looked to one another.

"You only had to ask. I would've helped you."

Charley faced me. "Thank you, dear, but this is something Ruth needed to do herself."

"I understand." Ruth seemed spent. Once the legal stuff was dealt with, she probably wanted to return to her life and forget about Belle and B&E charges.

The door opened, and Officer Hodkins walked toward me. My time was up. Then I noticed Maya behind him.

She sported a smile and hurried to my side. "Mrs. McGuffey agreed to drop the charges as long as neither of you step onto her property again."

The cop slid his key into the cell door.

"But…" Charley looked like someone poked her with a pin and let her air out. "What about proof?"

"Mom?" Maya pleaded.

Ruth shook her head. "No. I'm done. I just want to go

home to Frank."

Officer Hodkins opened the cell door, and escorted the women out. "You'll need to sign paperwork and get your belongings at the front desk."

I winked my thanks and followed Charley, Ruth, and Maya. As much as Ruth wanted to go home and pretend, I had a feeling Charley would convince her otherwise. And this wasn't the end of it.

* * *

After a fitful nights' sleep, which was beginning to become the norm for me, I hit a drive-through Starbucks on the way to the office, my mind focused on a single task today: find out what Mayor Brumhill had been up to three years ago.

Maya was hanging up the phone as I entered. She looked up and gave a sleepy smile. "Hey boss. Thanks for last night. Or this morning. It was really nice of you to help her out."

She had no idea how nice. It had almost killed me to have to utter the words "rain check" to Aiden again, before shooing him out of my place. But if my mother had been in the same situation, I'm sure Maya would have dropped everything, too.

"How are things now?" I asked.

She puffed up her chest and let out a long breath. "I think Mom's done playing detective. Ruth definitely wants nothing to do with it anymore. I'll be surprised if she talks to Mom for the next couple of days."

"I'm glad it worked out, and if you need anything, just ask, okay?"

She nodded.

The conference room door opened, and Sam and Caleigh walked over to us. "Have you heard from Danny? Any dates with Phillip planned?" Sam asked.

"Not yet. I have something I need you girls to do for me first."

"Is everything alright?" The corners of Caleigh's mouth lowered.

"It will be."

I'd made the decision last night that as much as I wanted to keep my personal life private, I needed back-up on this case. If Maya could handle having her crazy mother call me in the middle of the night from prison, I could handle the girls knowing that my father's shooter might be alive, well, and possibly within our grasp to put behind bars. I quickly filled them in on the way Aiden had found the gun that shot Derek, and how I'd been looking into the case. I purposely left Derek's involvement vague. If it turned out that he really had been involved in something shady, the last thing I wanted was for them to be culpable. When I was done, Sam said, "What do you need us to do, boss?"

My heart swelled, as corny as that sounded. They hadn't questioned why I'd been keeping it a secret, hadn't been shocked or hurt. My girls rocked. "I need as much information as you can find on our ex-mayor. I also need to know who this is."

I held out a printed photo of the meth head. It was pixilated, but hopefully they could do something with it."

"On it," said Caleigh, grabbing the photo. "Got any more to go on? Like, where this was taken or by whom?"

I bit my lip. As much as I loved them.. no, *because* I loved them, the less they knew the better. "No. Just the photo."

Caleigh nodded. "Okay, boss, I'll do my best."

"Don't worry," Sam said. "We'll find all the dirt."

* * *

I left the girls hard at work, flipped through my messages, answered a few emails from clients, then, once I'd waited an appropriate amount of time for the morning to drag by, made my way to Danny's. Predictably, he was still asleep when I arrived. He answered the door shirtless, wearing a pair of sweats that hung low on his hips. His hair mussed, his eyes heavy, features still soft with sleep. He looked vulnerable that way, and oddly enticing.

"Hey," he said, yawning as he held the door open. "Want coffee?"

"Always," I responded.

"Five minutes." Danny turned and shuffled to his

kitchen.

I hung back in the living room, sitting on his mustard-colored sofa. Danny's idea of interior design meant one quality piece of furniture in each room, and camera equipment everywhere else.

"What's up?" Danny asked, coming back with two cups a few minutes later. "To what do I owe this early morning visit?"

"It's ten-thirty."

"I was up late."

"Doing?" I asked.

Danny grinned and opened his mouth to speak.

"Wait!" I held up a hand. "Strike that. I don't want to know." Despite my words, my gaze strayed to his bare torso, the waistband of his sweats, and what I now knew lay beneath.

"Relax. I was alone last night. I'm saving myself for you, Bond," he said with a playful wink.

I cleared my throat, feeling my cheeks heat despite his teasing tone. "Did Phillip call you yet?" I asked, sipping at my coffee to cover any inappropriate thoughts that might try to enter my brain.

He shook his head. "Nope. Not yet."

"Can you call him?"

"Now?" Did I detect a note of a whine in his voice?

"Come on, Danny, you can't get the dirt if you don't see him."

A nervous expression flitted across his features.

"You just need to connect with him one more time, and he'll probably hit on you." I wasn't sure that last part would propel him into action, so I decided to change the subject and play into his male ego.

"I know it was difficult for you, but you did a great job." I added a super cheesy grin for reassurance.

He ran his hand through his hair, making it stand on end even further. Strangely, it didn't detract from his appeal any.

"Maybe you can think of it as calling up a pal for lunch," I offered. Of course that wouldn't get us to point B as quickly as asking him on a date, but if it got Danny to pick up the damn phone, then we were moving one step forward. "Besides, the quicker you catch him hitting on you, the faster this whole ordeal will be done, and you can go back to using your skills on the fairer sex."

His expression shifted. I hadn't a clue what he was thinking, but something got through because he walked to the coffee table and picked up his cell. He scrolled, which meant he was serious enough to program in Phillip's number, then dialed. He didn't hold it to his ear but out so I could hear.

I stood and walked to his side.

It rang twice. "Hello?"

"Hey, Phillip, it's me, Danny. From Cock..." Danny winced. "From the club last night."

"Yeah, I remember. How could I forget?" Phillip chuckled.

Danny joined in, but I could tell his version was fake. "So I was wondering if you're available today?"

"Oh yeah?" Phillip sounded hesitant.

I nudged Danny's arm. He frowned at me. We couldn't lose this opportunity. Danny would have to put on the charm, or the girls and I would have to spend countless hours tailing this guy. And I didn't have that kind of time right now.

"How about lunch?" Danny said. "We could discuss your portfolio."

That was all Phillip needed. "Actually, that sounds great. Um, I can't today though. What about tomorrow before my shift. Breakfast maybe?"

Danny looked to me. I nodded.

"Yeah, that'll work," he said, then listened as Philip rattled off a time and place.

I silently cheered, arms raised to the ceiling, swaying my hips.

Danny stared at them, gave me a wink. I stuck my tongue out at him.

"Great. I'll call you later, and we can finalize it. I'm on my way into an audition."

"Okay. Break a leg."

They hung up, and I squeezed Danny's bicep. "See, that wasn't so hard."

Danny shook his head, tossed his phone onto a sofa cushion, and picked up his coffee. "The things I do for you,

Bond."

I decided to leave him alone before he changed his mind. "So, we'll mic you before the lunch, okay?"

He grunted. "Hey, you still owe me," he told me as I headed for the door. "And trust me, I plan on cashing in big time."

I bit my lip. Oh, boy.

I quickly let myself out before he could voice just what he had in mind. As I crossed the street to my car, my cell rang. The caller ID said it was the office.

"Hello?"

"Boss." Sam sounded panicked.

My body grew alert, my mind going immediately to Brumhill as I flung open my car door. "What's wrong? What did you find?"

"Nothing. I mean, we're still looking into that. But Maya just got a call from her mother and someone named Ruth."

Oh, this wouldn't be good. "What happened?"

"Maya told me not to bother you with it, but because she specifically said *not* to tell you, I figured you'd want to know."

What was with the Alexander women and wanting to keep everything a secret? "I do. What's going on?"

"Something about her mother and Ruth in Belle's house."

I closed my eyes and thought a really dirty word. I *so* did not have time for this today.

"I heard Maya rattle off the address. You want it?" Sam asked.

I slammed my door shut and turned on the ignition. My girls were the highest paid PI's for a reason. "Hit me."

# CHAPTER FIFTEEN

———

I parked out in front of Belle McGuffey's single-story, ranch style home and ran up the wide driveway, past a shiny red Cadillac. Home-wrecker aside, the woman had great taste. The front door stood ajar, and shrill voices permeated through the thin opening.

"Mom, this has become insane. Put it down," Maya shrieked.

"Not until she admits it."

I pushed the door open wider and stepped into the house. Maya stood a couple of feet ahead of me. She'd clutched her hands into fists and stood with her feet wide apart, as if her shoes had been glued to the tile.

Charley was in the living room, near the fireplace, in the same position Maya stood, but holding an aluminum baseball bat.

The woman I assumed was Belle was across the room from her, on her knees, one arm around Ruth's neck in a choke hold. Ruth's face didn't look strained, as if she wasn't getting air, but she obviously wasn't comfortable either.

What the hell were they thinking?

"Are you all crazy?" I shouted, imagining the police arriving any second and handcuffing all of us. Not a bad thing since Charley and Belle had obviously lost all sense of sanity and deserved it.

They glanced my way.

"Boss, what are you doing here?" Maya's frown deepened.

"Jamie, this doesn't concern you," Charley said, attention back on her prey.

"It absolutely concerns me." Especially when I've driven

to the police station after midnight and rushed through midday traffic to make sure everyone was unharmed. I took a step toward them.

"Stay back." Belle's bark caused me to flinch and stop moving. Now I understood Maya's baseball mound stance.

"Why are you both doing this?" I immediately went into negotiator mode.

Charley wiggled her bat at her friend. "She's threatened to snap Ruth's neck."

Belle was wire thin. Her biceps appeared to have the strength of a mosquito. Ruth had forty pounds on her captor. She could've easily wrestled free.

"You broke into my house. Again." Belle's shriek made me wince. This woman had full range of her vocal chords.

"Mom, you promised you'd stay away."

Charley tightened her grip on the bat. "Things changed, pumpkin."

"What changed?" I took a small step forward.

Charley stared at her friend. "Tell them."

Ruth flailed her arms then pointed to her neck.

Belle, noticing, loosened her grip. "Oh, sorry."

I glanced at Maya, who gave me the same puzzling look I felt. This was like a bad *Saturday Night Live* skit.

Ruth cleared her throat. "When I got home last night, Frank wasn't there."

"She called his cell, and this tart answered," Charley shouted.

Belle puffed up her cheeks. "I am not a tart."

"She called me, hysterical, for which, of course, I don't blame her. Do you see what the tart is wearing?"

Belle had on an ankle-length, rose-colored, silk robe. She was covered from head to toe, not an inch of skin showing.

"Well, was he here?" I asked, trying to get back on point. I was pretty certain insulting the crazy woman holding your friend hostage wasn't a great idea.

Ruth sniffled. "No."

"Where is he?"

Charley jabbed the air with the bat. "She won't tell us."

"Because I don't know. I haven't seen Frank since last

night. He must've left his phone here. I found it in the sofa cushions. When it rang, I answered. I didn't think it would start World War Three."

I pinched the bridge of my nose, trying to hold my patience in check. I didn't want to shoot off at the mouth and insult them. Charley and Ruth seemed like genuinely nice women, but there were some loose screws. "This isn't the way to get answers. If Frank isn't here, there's no reason to assume..."

"You're all insane," Maya shouted, choosing the undiplomatic route. "I should just call the police and have you arrested. Again."

Ruth's face paled.

Charley's mouth gaped open, her bat hold loosened. "You wouldn't."

"Why not? Maybe actually staying in jail and having a record would show you that you can't break into people's homes."

"Technically the front door was open," Belle said. "I burned the toast and was airing out the house."

Whose side was she on?

Maya ignored her. "You're not a PI, Mom. This isn't the right way to investigate something. Right, Jamie?"

"Uh...um." I sputtered, unaware she was going to fling me into her point. "Absolutely. A good PI stays on the positive side of the law."

"But Remington and David..."

"Mom, that's television." Maya stormed over to her mother and snatched the bat from her hands. Well that was easy.

Charley pointed to Ruth and pouted.

"Oh, sorry." Belle released Ruth, and both women hauled themselves to their feet with the help of the sofa back.

"So are we good here now?" I expected Belle to mention pressing charges again, and I didn't think Maya would try to convince her otherwise this time.

"I still don't know where Frank is or if..." Ruth turned to Belle. "Are you sleeping with my husband?"

Belle curled a lock of her long, dark hair around a finger. "No. Not yet."

Oh, snap.

Ruth picked up a vase of yellow tulips and threw it at Belle.

The vase bounced off the throw rug, still in one piece, but the flowers flew out, scattering across the floor, and the water soaked the bottom of Belle's robe.

Charley cheered.

Maya gave her a long, stern stare.

Belle picked up a sofa pillow and tossed it at Ruth. "He's a great man. And he's bored. You don't show him any attention."

The pillow landed at Ruth's feet. She grabbed a magazine from the coffee table and zinged it at Belle, like a Frisbee. "Lie." But from the worried look on Ruth's face, I wasn't convinced she believed her words.

"Who do you think you are?" Charley hissed her words, grabbing a small geranium from a side table and flinging it toward Belle.

Ruth ducked, and it whizzed past her, falling in a cloud of dirt beside Belle. Charley had a great arm. Now I understood why she chose a bat as a weapon.

"Mom, stay out of it."

"No, I won't. And stop talking to me like I'm a child. Would you stay out of it if Jamie was in trouble?"

Maya glanced at me then lowered her gaze. "No."

A smile tugged one corner of my mouth. The feeling was mutual, and put into that context, I suddenly saw Charley and Ruth in a new light. Still crazy, but it made more sense.

"He's married. You can't have him." Ruth reached for the fireplace and grabbed an urn. She raised it over her head.

Belle screamed, "No."

Ruth froze and glanced up. Realizing it wasn't a lidded vase and probably contained the ashes of a dead man, a dead husband, she gently lowered her arms, placed the urn back on the mantle, and swiped a small framed photo instead.

Belle ducked, and it sailed through the archway, hitting a bowl of bananas on the dining table. The fruit jumped but remained in the bowl. The frame bounced and crashed onto the floor. Glass shattered.

Charley, Maya, and I cringed.

Belle picked up the tulips and threw them, one at a time,

stems first. They didn't come close to hitting Ruth. "Do you think once you have that piece of paper you don't have to try anymore? No more seduction. No more wooing. That's the perfect way to kill a relationship." Her eyes grew misty. Was she still talking about Ruth and Frank or her dead spouse?

Charley made some unrecognizable sound. I knew she had to sympathize with Belle.

"Frank needs attention, and if you won't give it to him, I will." She lifted her chin in defiance.

Ruth gasped but didn't respond. The room grew quiet. Too quiet.

Then Ruth stepped forward, raised her arm, and slapped Belle across the face. The sound echoed. "He's mine, and you won't get him."

She turned and marched past us, out the front door. She appeared strong and in control for the first time since we'd met.

Charley smiled and followed, adding a, "hmm" as she strode by.

Maya turned from the open door and back to Belle, who was holding her cheek. "I'm terribly sorry. I'll make sure they won't bother you again. For sure this time."

"Just go."

Maya grabbed my hand, and we ran out.

*  *  *

After reassuring Maya it was fine if she took the rest of the day off to spend time with her mother and Ruth, I headed back to the office. Maya said her notes on Brumhill were on her desk, so I stopped there first and found a legal pad with her perfect, loopy penmanship. Beneath his name, she'd written his current address and other statistical information. He was an Aries, lived in Malibu, and drove a black sports car. All very mundane and typical for an aging politician.

The printer hummed, causing me to flinch.

Sam walked from the conference room and grabbed the sheets of paper. "Hey boss, how'd it go with Maya's mom? Anything serious?"

I wasn't sure how much Maya wanted anyone else to

know, but I was done with secrets for the day. "They're fine. A friend is going through a rough patch in her marriage. They'll work it out."

At least I hoped they would. One less divorce statistic sounded great right now. "I told her to take the rest of the day off. We can man the phones, right?"

On cue, Caleigh entered the reception area. She wore Maya's Bluetooth and spoke into the air. "Yes, it sounds like you made the right choice in calling us."

It looked like they already had everything under control. As usual.

Caleigh wiggled her brows at me, then sat at Maya's desk, opening the scheduling software. "Let's see, how about next Tuesday, at two. Is that a good time to come in?"

Sam and I moved out of ear shot, into my office. We sat in the two chairs facing my desk.

"So we dug as far back as we could on Brumhill," Sam whispered.

Oh, no, this didn't sound promising.

She handed over the pages she'd just printed. I looked through them as she explained what I was reading, although they seemed pretty straightforward. Checking and savings account information, credit history, homes owned…my girls were as accurate and lethal as the CIA, but much better dressed.

"He has no criminal charges, not even sexual inappropriateness in the workplace. He's never even gotten a speeding ticket."

My hope and shoulders slumped with each word she uttered.

"He's been married for fifty-two years. No complaints of domestic violence, and he always remembers his wife's birthday and anniversary."

He was a saint.

"They have two grown children. Both girls. Both married with their own families. The youngest married a politician who's currently running for governor in Richmond, and the eldest is a pediatrician in Seattle."

And raised saints.

"Nothing has ever tainted his political career. We

couldn't even find a suggested taint."

I sighed and rubbed the space between my brows. This wasn't helping the headache that seemed determined to spearhead me.

"Sorry," Sam said.

I patted her hand. "No, this is great. Really."

Normally, I'd assume I'd just been wrong. I'm woman enough to admit that it happened from time to time. But I'd seen the tape. That was definitely Brumhill driving the car, and he handed the meth head money for something. Whatever the payoffs were for, they'd been covered up well. "What about the guy in the photo?"

Sam whistled and raised her brows. "He's another story. Richie Campbell." She handed me a very lengthy, handwritten rap sheet.

"He's been arrested numerous times for drug possession and selling, in and out of a school zone, which worsens the offense. He's a member of the *Los Leones*, a gang that operates out of Compton, and he's currently incarcerated in San Quentin, for the next twelve years."

"When did he go to jail?'

Reading sideways, Sam trailed a finger down the page in my lap. "Three years ago on April thirtieth. But he was arrested on the eleventh."

The day after Derek's shooting. Was Campbell my father's shooter?

\* \* \*

By the time I reached the marina, nightfall was approaching. Red, orange, and gold ribbons stretched across the horizon, kissing the top of the water. From the parking lot, I'd noticed Derek on the top deck. I climbed the short ladder, remembering to take off my pumps first. When I reached the top, I stuffed my shoes into my purse and hedged around to the empty lounge chair, beside him.

"You look exhausted," he said, holding out a beer from an ice chest.

I sank into the creaky seat and gladly took the ice cold

bottle. "I could sleep for days."

"Anything new on the gay man?"

I narrowed a glance at him. How did he know that?

He leaned over, popped the top off my beer with a bottle opener in the shape of breasts, and flashed a devilish grin. It was the one that made the ladies weak. It was dazzling. Too bad I was his daughter and it meant nothing. "I spoke with Caleigh earlier. It's about time Danny put his charm to use."

I took a long swallow of the bubbly beverage then closed my eyes. "I'm not quite sure he'd agree."

"Ah, he should be thrilled to work alongside such a success."

I opened one eye. "Oh, boy, that's laying it on thick. What do you want?"

He chuckled. "Me? You're the one who's visiting."

I turned my attention to the sunset.

"And the one who sent those girls to drag me off my boat."

I froze. He knew?

"Did you find whatever you were looking for?"

I swallowed hard then took another swig of beer. He sounded so calm. Was this a test? I considered lying or playing dumb, but he was right in more than one way about the exhaustion. I wanted the truth, and that meant I needed to play it straight.

"What happened after you filmed Brumhill paying Campbell?"

The silence was electric.

"Look, we can sit here and pretend I didn't snoop and you aren't keeping secrets, but we'll both know we're lying. This is getting old. Just tell me already, Dad. Please."

I wasn't sure if it was the 'please' or the 'dad' that finally won his heart, but he turned to me and finally said, "I gave a copy of the tape to Brady."

# CHAPTER SIXTEEN

———

We moved below, into the galley, away from possible eavesdroppers. Plus, being on the top deck was a bit dangerous when you combined the dark sky with high heels and alcohol. We settled at the table. Derek leaned forward, elbows on the Formica. He looked pained, like his pants were too tight after a big, extravagant meal.

I considered making coffee but didn't want to derail this conversation. Plus I kinda valued my internal organs. Drinking that sludge would surely kill them. Instead I reached into the cooler he'd set on the floor, and grabbed a second beer.

He quirked an eyebrow. "Aren't you driving? Or do you plan on spending the night?"

And be privy to the sounds of him and tonight's bed partner? No thank you. I set the bottle down.

He grabbed it, popped the top, and guzzled half of it in one gulp. "You were right about Brady and me. We were buddies. In fact, he was one of few cops I ever considered a friend, even a close one."

I imagined them at the bar, chatting about their days on the streets wrangling criminals and cheating spouses. In my experience, cops didn't take PIs too seriously. They must've connected on some other level as well.

"What happened?"

"I'd been following Bernstein. His wife hired me to catch him cheating. One night I watched a young man leave Bernstein's office building, get into a car, and hand the driver money."

I knew this part but didn't want to stop his flow, so I remained quiet. I leaned back in my seat and tried to relax, but the tension in my neck and shoulders was too tight.

"I recognized Brumhill immediately, but had to tail the young guy to find out he was a drug dealer. Campbell."

I knew it was silly to worry about Derek. He was more seasoned than I, and more stubborn. Maybe. But the idea of him nosing around in gang territory made my skin itch. After the shooting, I guess I saw him as weak and in need of protecting. If he ever knew I thought of him that way, he'd be crushed. And I'd be the one in need of protection.

"It happened several times over a few days."

This was new information. "But I only saw one surveillance tape."

He smirked. "The others are hidden elsewhere. Just in case."

In case he died that night. I pinched the bridge of my nose to keep my impending headache at bay.

"So, what happened?"

"I figured out that Bernstein was facilitating cover-ups between our ex-Mayor and a drug cartel. Anytime one of the members was too stupid and got caught by the cops, Bernstein would go through the legal motions, but Brumhill would grease the wheels so no one got convicted."

Which meant that this corruption extended into the justice system, too. Great. More of our tax dollars keeping the criminals on the street.

"What did Brumhill get out of this? I mean, it was a huge risk."

"It was. But it was financing Brumhill's campaigns. He needed the cash, believe it or not. Honest money is hard to come by in politics."

That I did believe. "But he's retired."

"Now. I imagine he has vacation homes in a couple of exotic locations."

Everything was sliding into place in my brain, except... "So you...did what?"

"I didn't know where to turn, who to trust. I knew Brumhill had to have several inside people on the take. So I gave copies of everything to the one guy I thought I could trust."

Brady.

"I didn't know what he would do with the information after that," he went on. "I figured he'd get it into the right hands, slip it to IA or something. Go high enough up the chain that Brumhill couldn't pay everyone off. I had no idea he'd kill Bernstein."

I stared into Derek's eyes. A deep frown had practically swallowed them. I reached forward and squeezed his fingers. "You couldn't have known. But you should've told me everything."

"I couldn't. I was trying to keep you safe." His voice cracked.

"Me? I wasn't involved."

"And I wanted to keep it that way. If you knew, you wouldn't have let it go."

He was right. I definitely would've taken action.

"Look, James, after Bernstein died, the tapes never surfaced. A lot of people are invested in making sure it stays that way. Brady and I, we're what you'd call loose ends. Brady's about to go away for life. You think I wanted my daughter putting the target on her back?"

I shook my head. "But don't you want it off yours?"

Derek laughed. "As long as I keep my damned mouth shut, Bernstein's death is the biggest of my sins." His laugh died on that last thought, the frown pulling at his eyes again.

"You couldn't have known," I repeated. "Maybe Brady didn't even set out to shoot Bernstein. I mean, maybe he's telling the truth and Bernstein came there with the gun."

He leaned back in his seat to ponder.

"Do you think Brady shot you?" I asked.

"I didn't before Aiden told you the gun that killed Bernstein was also used to shoot me. Now I'm not so sure."

"It definitely looks incriminating, but it's possible Bernstein brought it to Brady's house…"

"To shoot Brady," Derek finished for me. "Maybe Brady took the info to Bernstein or even Brumhill and tried blackmailing them, and they wanted him out of the way."

I nodded. We were going down the same road. "And not only did they find out that Brady knew but you did, too."

We sat quiet in our satisfaction for a moment. Until

Derek said, "Or Brady's lying and he killed Bernstein for any number of reasons, not the least of which could have been he was on the take, too."

"You think Brumhill thought Bernstein was a loose end?"

Derek shrugged. "Who knows. Bernstein was facilitating the pay-offs, but he was just a pawn. Easy to replace."

"Or maybe Brady thought he was taking justice into his own hands," I said, remembering the news articles I'd read about him.

Derek nodded. "He was a bit of a loose cannon back then."

"He still is." Reluctantly, I told him about Brady surprising me in my car after work.

His face reddened. "Did he touch you?"

"No. He was just trying to scare me." Looking back on it, I believed what I said. If he'd wanted to hurt me, he would've done so. He had plenty of opportunity.

"What did Aiden have to say about that? And why didn't the cops revoke his bail? Don't tell me he's paying someone off now."

I shook my head. "I never called the police or told Aiden."

His eyebrows nearly jumped off his face. "Since when don't you follow the law?"

"Seriously? Do you know me at all? I may not be greasing palms to get what I want, but a little innocent B&E to gather evidence never hurt anyone. I am your daughter after all."

He smiled full and proud. "Yes, you are."

I thought of Charley and Ruth. They'd only wanted proof of an affair. If it had been my husband, I would've done the same thing. Except I would've waited until Belle wasn't home. Then again, I also would've confronted the husband first. With the baseball bat for insurance.

"Unfortunately, we may never know what really happened to Bernstein," Derek said, interrupting my thoughts.

And that's where the fork in the road appeared, and while he veered to the left, I ventured to the right. There was no way in hell I was taking not knowing as an option. I'd get some answers, even if it meant hog-tying Brumhill and delivering water torture until he spilled. No more mysteries.

* * *

After parking my car, I walked to the front steps of my building and was surprised to find Aiden sitting there, waiting for me. It was as if we were on the same wave length, and he knew how draining my day had been.

Out of his usual designer suit collection, he wore dark, fitted jeans and a T-shirt. His hair was still perfectly gelled in place. Not for long though. I planned on getting my fingers in there and messing up his hard work.

"Well, you're a nice surprise," I told him.

"I wanted to see you."

I smiled, probably displaying my molars. "The feeling's mutual," I said, totally meaning it. "You want to come up?"

"I'm not sure that's a good idea." Aiden gave me a wan smile, and my radar perked up. That was not the expression of a guy excited about the prospect of a hot night with a hot girl.

"Okay. What's up?" I asked, almost not wanting to hear an answer.

Aiden cleared his throat. "I spent the day going over notes and working on the case, but I couldn't concentrate. Thoughts of you and the other night kept interjecting."

I nodded. He was thinking about me. That was a good thing, right? So why did I feel like something bad was about to come out of his mouth. "The other night was fun," I said, trying to lighten the suddenly heavy mood.

Aiden nodded. "It was. Fun."

It sounded like a "but" should follow, but he didn't say a word. Finally I couldn't take it anymore.

"But?"

"But I don't think I should come up tonight."

He'd already said that. And that was when I knew something was really wrong. Aiden didn't fumble with his words. Words were his weapons, his skills of the trade. If he was grasping for them now, something was up.

My chest squeezed out a heavy breath. I sat beside him.

Neither of us said a word. I stared up at the sky and tried to focus on the stars, but as I waited for him to clue me in, I ran through the possibilities. He was moving back to Kansas City. His old job offered him a raise, and he was leaving as soon as Brady's case was done. Or was it something about Brady's case? Had he found something more about the gun? About Derek's connection to Brady? If he knew I was holding out on him, I wasn't sure he'd be jumping at the chance to play tonsil hockey with me again.

A horn honked down the street. Shouts were heard from inside my building. A woman yelled at her husband to lower the TV. Typical sounds yet they gnawed at my composure.

"There's something going on. Just go ahead and tell me. Are you leaving L.A.?" I asked.

He frowned for a second. "No, nothing like that. I love my job. I'm getting used to the city. And I love my…new friends."

I raised an eyebrow his way. Was that supposed to refer to me? "Then what is it? Why did you want to see me? Because I'm getting the feeling it's not for my hot little dress tonight?"

There was that wan smile again. "I'm having a hard time of it."

"The case? It's understandable…"

He shook his head. "Not the case."

I held my breath. Aiden cleared his throat. The tension was thick enough to cut with a stiletto.

"Look, the other night was fun…"

"You already said that," I cut in.

More throat clearing. "Right. It was more than fun. It felt good, exciting. Something I haven't felt in a long time."

I felt that "but" hanging in the air again. "Go on."

"It just didn't feel right."

And there it was.

I stared out at the street where the tenants parked. The row of cars blurred. It was amazing how quickly my body reacted to this new development, yet my mind hadn't caught up yet. My throat constricted, and I told myself to ignore it. I mean, it wasn't as if he'd proposed and was taking back the ring. It was one night of lip-lock.

"Look, it's not you," he said quickly, the words flooding out now. "I like you, Jamie. I honestly do. I've enjoyed getting to know you, spending time with you. You're smart, beautiful, interesting."

I couldn't help an ironic laugh at how all my wonderful traits were surfacing as he dumped me.

"Wow, I sound like a catch," I said, painfully aware that sarcasm was not one of my more attractive traits.

"You are," Aiden said, the sincerity in his voice the polar opposite to my statement. "I just couldn't stop thinking about…her."

"Her?" I jumped on the word, turning to him.

"Sarah," he said quietly.

Shit. "Your wife."

He nodded. "I thought I was ready to move on, but…I don't know. As much as I wanted to be there with you the other night, she was still somehow there, too. And that's not fair. To either of us."

He was still in mourning for his dead wife. As much as I wanted to hate him for the brush-off I was getting, I couldn't. I knew what it felt like to lose someone you loved. I took in a deep breath. "It's only been a year," I reasoned. "It's not like you can erase her from your life."

A corner of his mouth tugged up for a moment then fell back into place. "I know. I just…I don't know how long it's going to take before I'm really ready to move on. If I'm ever ready."

"But I'm not the first person you've seen since Sarah passed away, right? You mentioned something about a date or two back home."

He nodded. "Yes, but that was different."

"How?"

"It was casual."

"And this wasn't?" I wasn't sure if I was happy or disappointed at the idea that this could have really been something. Though at this point, I guess it didn't matter which.

Aiden didn't answer, just sent that wan smile my way again. Part regret, part guilt. It should have pissed me off, but all it did was make me want to drag him upstairs and comfort him that much more.

"So, this is it," I said, my chest tight. "The classic it's-not-you-it's-me."

"You know it's not like that," Aiden said, his voice thick. "Look, I want this, Jamie. You have no idea how badly I want to come upstairs with you right now."

For a moment, I totally believed him.

"But it's selfish of me to go down that road with you when I don't know if I'll ever be able to really move on. If I'll ever be able to be with you without feeling guilty that I'm with you, then guilty for thinking about her." He took a deep breath. "I'm sorry."

"Me too." On instinct I reached out and took his hand. It was warm, his palm sweating. His fingers wrapped gratefully around mine. I didn't know what he was talking about, because from my end, his hand in mine felt totally right. I wanted to be with him, he wanted to be with me. But there was just one little dead woman in the middle of it all. It was hard to compete with that.

We sat like that in silence for several seconds before I finally stood, taking my hand with me. "Well, I guess I'll see you around the courthouse then, counselor."

Aiden stood too, his eyes heavy with all the regret and guilt he'd just confessed to. "Absolutely," he promised. He paused. "Jamie, this isn't goodbye, it's just—"

"See you around," I finished for him before I could read any false hope into whatever he was about to say next. Then I turned and bolted up the stairs.

# CHAPTER SEVENTEEN

———

Danny paced in the lobby, running his hands through his hair. I sat in clear view of him from my desk. He'd just arrived, hadn't even said hi yet. The girls were applying their spy gear, which included cameras, microphones, and pouty lip gloss. Danny and Phillip were meeting for breakfast at the same cafe Aiden and I had shared the other day. I cringed at the thought, but refused to let myself wallow.

I clicked off the report I was writing about this case thus far and gathered my purse. As much as I was dying to dig into Brumhill today, when Danny had called with the details of his "date," I'd had to put it on the back burner. A fact that made me both anxious and jumpy this morning. And the four cups of coffee I'd downed didn't help much.

Between Derek's revelations and Aiden's surprise visit, I'd spent the evening torn between crying jags and cursing the stupidity of men in general. But one thing was certain. I was sick of it all. All of the games, all of the lies, and all of the nice-guy fronts hiding misdeeds. Whoever had shot Derek better watch their back because I was one blonde who was short on sleep, short on nerves, and short on patience for the less-fair sex today.

Danny stopped pacing when he saw me walk into the lobby and grabbed my wrist, tugging me close. "Maybe we should call this off."

"We've been through this. You can do it," I told him. I so did not need him backing out on me today. "Just picture him as one of those redheads you're so fond of."

He swatted my words with his hand. "That's not it."

I sighed. "Then what?"

"I'm talking about trying to ruin his marriage."

It took me a full five seconds to rewire my thoughts. "Whoa, where did that come from?"

He glanced at Maya, who was on the phone, not paying us any attention. "Phillip called me last night. We got to talking. He's a nice guy."

"And?"

"And nothing." He combed his fingers through his hair, making it stick out at the ends. "We talked about stuff."

I narrowed my eyes. "What kind of stuff?"

He shrugged. "You know, baseball, cars, current events."

I lifted my brows. Where was he going with this? "Anything pertinent to the case?"

"He mentioned he'd been sneaking out, keeping something from Craig, but when I pressed him why, he changed the subject."

"Where did he call you from?"

"He was home. Craig was working late, and Phillip was bored."

"Bored? Come on, he didn't hit on you, talk dirty? Maybe a little phone sex?"

He grimaced and reddened under his tan. "It's not like that. We've become friends."

"Well, it sounds like your friend has already confessed that he's stepping out on his husband. So, I'd say we're not the ones ruining his marriage. He is."

"He's a good guy. I just don't want to mess up his life."

Danny was falling for him. Not in a romantic way, but Phillip still managed to ooze enough charm to win Danny's friendship. Damn, this could make it harder to get what we needed. "Look. One of the rules of PI work is to never get emotionally close to a mark or a client. It clouds judgment and makes the job so much harder."

He nodded, but I didn't see my words register in his eyes.

"You know, if Phillip's cheating then Craig deserves to know. And if Phillip's unhappy in the marriage, then he deserves to get out and find what makes him happy." And hopefully this morning that would be a six-foot-two photographer with pale blue-green eyes.

"You're right."

Of course I was. I patted him on the shoulder. "Don't worry. It'll all work out fine." But as Danny nodded again and turned away, I bit my lower lip. What if this lunch was a disaster? What if Danny couldn't get what we needed due to his new attachment? From now on, we needed to keep him behind the camera and leave the PI work to the licensed, trained professionals.

As if on cue, the front doors opened and Charley walked in.

Uh-oh.

Maya rushed from around her desk as I approached. "What are you doing here, Mom? Is everything alright? Where's Ruth? Is Belle dead?"

I wanted to laugh at her last inquiry, but my brain was too wound in knots to remember how.

Charley caressed her daughter's hand. "Everything is fine, dear. Ruth's home with Frank, and Belle's still breathing. I assume. I haven't seen her."

She turned to me and reached out for my hand. I gripped her fingers, and she gave mine a tender squeeze. "I came by to let you both know we're all okay. And to apologize."

"So Ruth found Frank?" I asked.

She nodded. "He'd spent the night at work. They talked it all out. They've agreed to go to counseling."

Maya smiled. "That's great."

"Yes, I'm amazed Ruth agreed to it. She doesn't open up easily, especially to strangers. But she's being brave and got Frank to promise he'd stay away from Belle."

I took a deep breath. This was fantastic news.

"And I'm terribly sorry for my role in all of this. I was foolish and never meant to put anyone, either of you, in a dangerous situation. If Belle had a gun in her home, this may have ended very differently."

Neither Maya nor I said a word. Charley was right. We were lucky.

She raised her right hand in true Scouts honor, letting mine go. "I promise there will be no more investigating for me. I'm retiring my spy status."

Maya let out a loud sigh. "That's a great idea, Mom."

Charley grinned. "Besides, I won't have much time. I signed up for surfing classes. Two hours a day with a tanned, muscled man who looks like a Greek God."

"Mom?" Maya's voice rose an octave.

"What? I am only going to look. He teaches on weekends, in his little spare time. He's in medical school, wanting to become a pediatrician. Isn't that adorable?"

Maya narrowed her eyes, obviously suspicious of something.

"He'd be a wonderful son-in-law."

And there it was.

Charley winked.

Maya rolled her eyes.

* * *

The hostess directed the girls and me to a table outside, on the patio. Although I didn't care for baking in the sun, there was an awning, and I was more grateful we weren't seated at the table I'd shared with Aiden. The thought of him made my stomach sour. I grabbed a chair facing away from the spot, trying to focus on the task at hand. As I'd told Danny, emotion and PI work didn't mix. I needed to stay sharp today.

Danny sat two tables across from us, closer to the street. Close enough for adequate pictures, but too far to overhear without our microphones.

The server came to take our orders. I couldn't deal with deciding or the thought of putting much in my stomach. Luckily, he rattled off the daily special as grilled chicken frittata with a pesto lime dressing. We ordered three and a pot of coffee

It was moderately busy, writers and agents comprising most of the clientele, doing early meetings and spreading their scripts out on the tables. It was almost ten. There were several empty tables, and the chatter was a calm buzz, but mixed with traffic, it was hard to distinguish what anyone was saying unless they were seated beside you.

We sipped our waters. Anyone watching must've thought we hated one another because we didn't utter a word.

Phillip arrived at exactly ten. There was something attractive about a punctual man. When he walked over, Danny rose and they hugged. I mentally crossed my fingers that we'd get some butt squeezing action or even a kiss, but it was one of those guy hugs, where it was more pec-to-pec with a pat on the back.

Caleigh sighed. "Darn." Guess she'd been hoping for the same.

The server hurried over for their order.

"The daily special, please," Phillip said then pulled his phone from his pocket and laid it beside his silverware. He hadn't even looked at the menu or heard the special. Was he a regular or didn't care? He glanced at the phone twice while waiting on Danny to order. He was definitely preoccupied about something.

The hostess directed two young women to the table beside us. The three of us rolled our eyes. The last thing we needed was chatty neighbors. A quick glance to them showed they were either sisters or best, best friends. One a bleached blonde (her eyebrows were almost black) and the other a light brunette, both had identical chin-length bobs. They each wore black mini-skirts and an off-the-shoulder top. One in pink and the other red. The blonde wore black gladiator sandals, while her friend-slash-sister wore a pair of leopard strappy sandals, with two-inch heels, which were to-die-for. She had excellent taste.

"Why do you keep staring at your phone? Waiting to hear back from an audition?" Danny asked.

I turned my attention back to the men.

Phillip shrugged. "Something like that."

"That's not enough. Push harder," I whispered.

If he did, I didn't hear it. Our server arrived with our frittatas, then turned to take the next table's order. Two waters with lemon, and they were going to share a side of scrambled egg whites, no oil. Seriously?

"His batting score was horrible last season. I wouldn't be surprised if they find a way to kick him off the team," I heard Danny say.

"They can't just fire him, can they?"

"If we split it evenly, this lunch will leave us with just enough calories to have a can of soup for dinner," said the brunette while tapping along on some sort of calculator beside us.

The blonde nodded. "That's great. I think I'll have the chicken noodle. And we can split a yogurt for dessert. Yogurt is so good."

"I know, right?"

Sam placed a huge bite of mozzarella-melted chicken into her mouth, closed her eyes, and moaned. It was only slightly less orgasmic than that scene in *When Harry Met Sally*.

I held my napkin to my lips, hiding my pesto grin.

The two girls wrinkled their noses and faced one another.

"So what are your plans for tonight? Because I thought maybe we could catch a movie or something, you know, just the two of us?" Danny asked. His tone was just flirty enough. I tensed as I listened for the answer.

Phillip shrugged. "Um, yeah. Maybe. I kind of have plans…"

"I saw those shoes we wanted, the ones with the wedge heels, at DSW. They look just like the designer ones."

Dammit!

I leaned into my plate, almost getting pesto-lime sauce on my blouse. "What did Phillip say? Who does he have plans with?" I asked, hoping it was some hot young thing and we could do the tail and get this over with.

The girls shook their heads.

I growled. "I can't hear a damn thing."

Caleigh whispered, "I'm on it."

"We should run over there after lunch," the blonde said.

Caleigh fake coughed and sniffled, using her napkin to wipe under her nose. "I finally went to the doctor yesterday." She pretended she was talking low, but her voice was loud enough for a couple of tables to hear.

Playing along, I asked, "What did he say?"

"That's the crazy thing. He's not sure what's causing my rash."

The two young women stopped chatting and leaned their bodies toward us.

"Or my rapid weight gain."

The women visually gasped.

Sam snickered.

I pressed my lips together.

Caleigh widened her eyes. "And the worse part…" She coughed and sputtered. "He thinks it's contagious."

The young women leaned away from our table.

"Look." Caleigh lifted the hem of her skirt, showing her flawless thigh to us. The women couldn't see a thing, but a man to my left caught the action and smiled. I wasn't sure if he heard our conversation or not.

On cue, Sam covered her mouth with her hand and appeared frightened.

Then Caleigh turned her head and coughed several times in the women's direction. She hadn't covered her mouth, and I watched a drop of spittle fly onto their table.

Gross.

But effective. They scooted their chairs over, grimacing. The brunette called the server over and asked if they could sit inside.

Once they were gone, Caleigh winked. The girl was good.

I turned my attention back to the guys just as Phillip's phone rang. He held it to his ear. "Hello? Yes, this is Philip. Yes. Okay." A smile sprang onto his face. "Yes, absolutely. Monday at three. We'll be there. Thank you."

He hung up but held onto his phone.

"You look happy. Did you get a part?" Danny asked.

"Much better. Do you mind if we cut this short? I have to speak with Craig." He pulled out his wallet.

Danny glanced at us, looking confused and panicked. "Uh, can't you just call him?"

"No. This is face-to-face kind of news." He tossed a couple of bills onto the table.

"News? Good news, I hope?" Danny asked.

Phillip met his gaze, and from my angle he looked like he was going to bust. "It's that secret I've been keeping from him. I didn't want to say anything until I knew for sure." He paused. "I really should tell Craig first."

What was he talking about?

"Oh, what the heck. It's not like you and Craig are friends." He leaned into the table and grabbed Danny's wrist.

Surprisingly, Danny didn't flinch.

"Do you have any idea how hard it is for a gay couple to get a baby? The agencies like to pretend they're progressive, but they're not. At least not the ones I looked into. So I've been meeting with a friend of mine from Cock Tails who went the private adoption route. I didn't want Craig to know anything yet because, well, I didn't want to get his hopes up in case this was another dead end. But my friend just called. He talked to his lawyer, and he thinks there's a baby available."

I blinked. For once, I was speechless. A baby?

Phillip let go of Danny and scooted out his chair. "Don't worry. It's perfectly legal. No pay offs. They do overseas adoptions. Now, I gotta run and tell Craig."

"Wait. A baby?"

"Yeah, isn't it great?" He stood.

Danny did too. "This is about adopting?"

But if Phillip picked up on Danny's weirdness, he ignored it. "I promise we'll get together soon. You can come over and have dinner with me and Craig. It'll be fun. I'll call you. Bye."

"Bye."

We all watched Phillip pass our table, oblivious to our staring, and rush through the cafe.

I turned to Danny. Adoption. He wasn't cheating.

Danny's expression appeared an odd mix of dejection and relief. I knew exactly how he felt.

* * *

After the cafe, I raced to Brumhill's home in Malibu. Well, raced as fast as mid-day traffic would allow, which meant I was there in a mere two hours. The estate sprawled for several acres, high above the Pacific Ocean with a view to die for. Most of the terrain in this area was hills and natural foliage, but around this home emerald green grass and carefully groomed shrubs replaced the wild growth. A stone and wrought-iron fence separated the house from the road, but surprisingly the entrance wasn't gated. I took the circular drive straight to the three-car garage without being stopped.

A couple of men in green pants and matching shirts squatted in the bushes, pulling up weeds and speaking in rapid Spanish. They smiled as I stepped from my car.

"This is the Brumhill home, correct?"

They both nodded. The older man said, "*Si.*"

"Is Mr. Brumhill home?"

"*Si.*"

I started to climb the steps to the ornate double doors.

"But he is not there," the man stopped me, his English heavily accented.

"He's not?"

The man pointed off behind him. "He is at the stables."

Of course they had stables. Probably a petting zoo too. All financed with drug money. This was better though. Inside I'd probably be harassed by the hired help. Outdoors, there wouldn't be anyone to rush me off before speaking to him. "That way?"

The gardener stood up and brushed loose dirt from his knees. He smiled and walked with me to the side of the house. He pointed to a barn-like structure in the close distance. "There."

"*Gracias,*" I told him.

I headed off, across the expansive lawn. The right heel of my pink pumps sank into the soft grass. I yanked my foot to remove it. On tiptoes, I quickened my steps. When I reached the stables, I was mildly panting. I found Brumhill brushing a small brown colt on the far side. I recognized him immediately, though he looked like he'd aged a good ten years in the last three, his hair now much more salt than pepper. Guilt did that to you.

"Mr. Brumhill?"

He looked up, brush mid-air, narrowing his eyes. "Who are you?"

"Jamie Bond. I have a few questions if you have time." Not that I was leaving if he didn't, but diplomacy usually went a long way.

He turned back to the colt and resumed brushing its coat. "Bond? Do we have an appointment?"

I shook my head. "No. But you've probably met my father, Derek Bond."

He continued brushing, as if he wasn't even aware I stood there. Then finally, he said, "Ah, yes, the private investigator. I've heard of him."

*Yeah, I bet.*

He looked back at me, and his gaze roamed my body— slow and deliberate. "Is it a family business?"

"Something like that. He's beautiful." I nodded to the young horse.

"Do you know anything about horses?"

"No. I always wanted lessons though." In junior high I became obsessed with the idea of riding. It started after watching a movie about a teenage girl who fell in love with a stable boy. Her family forbade them from seeing one another. It was quite tortured and, of course, had a happy ending. Great pre-teen fodder.

"They are fine, strong creatures." Brumhill patted the colt's side and put the brush down. "So what can I do for you, Ms. Bond?"

I'd seen Brumhill on the news plenty of times, but I'd never paid close attention. He was just another politician making empty promises. Since his retirement he'd grown a beard— silvery-white and cropped short. It suited his round, almost elfish face. He stood several inches shorter than me, something I didn't expect.

"I'm looking into who shot my father, three years ago."

The sunlight made him squint. He raised a hand to shield his eyes. And obscure my ability to read his expression. "Sorry to hear that. Is he okay?"

"He's fine."

"You said three years ago. Isn't it a bit late to be investigating?"

"New evidence has surfaced."

"Oh?"

When I didn't offer more information, he busied himself with patting down the colt. "What does this have to do with me?"

This was the moment when I had to choose between blurting out all I truly knew, which meant accusing our ex-mayor of crimes, or putzing around to see what he may slip up and say. It was unlikely he'd been agonizing to clear his conscience, with his mansion and horses and hired gardeners, but going too indirect would get me nowhere. I chose to straddle both sides.

"The gun used to shoot my father was also used to kill an attorney named Bernstein."

He continued patting. It started out slow and gentle, then picked up speed. I was certain the colt wanted to kick him. He wasn't touching me and I wanted to. "Isn't that the cop trial?"

"Why, yes, it is," I said, faking surprise that he kept abreast of the tawdry scandals of a corrupt cop. But we both knew why I was really here. He had to have put the pieces together by now.

"You still haven't said what this has to do..."

With him? Yeah, yeah. "My father remembers seeing you at Mr. Bernstein's office one evening, shortly before he was killed."

This caused him to stop torturing the colt and give me his full attention. "I visited lots of people's offices three years ago. I was the mayor back then. I'm not sure I understand—"

"After office hours?" I interrupted. "It was dark when you were...spotted." No sense in letting him know there was video.

"The mayor doesn't keep nine-to-five hours." His mouth was tight now, tension present.

"Funny you don't remember it," I said. "Considering the case has been all over the news, and Bernstein's name is practically on everyone's lips, I'd think your memory would have been jogged by now."

Brumhill stared at me, his eyes dark and unreadable. For a small man he suddenly had a large presence, and I could easily see how he had commanded one of the largest cities in the country.

"Whatever my dealings, young lady," he finally said, his voice tight and even, "I guarantee they had nothing to do with your father's shooting and are none of your business. You may leave now." He stood straight and centered, with all his weight evenly distributed on his feet.

Part of me wanted to refuse. Who was he going to get to physically remove me? One of the gardeners?

We stared at one another, and the longer I didn't budge,

the more blank his expression grew. If he was guilty, he should've gone into acting. If he was innocent of trying to kill Derek, then I'd just made another enemy. C'est la vie!

I flashed a grin. "Thank you for your time."

I turned and headed back to my car. The sun beat on my head. Sweat trickled behind my ears. But the burning sensation that ran along my back had nothing to do with the sun and everything to do with Brumhill's stare. I refused to turn around to give him the satisfaction of meeting it though. I nodded good-bye to the gardeners and settled into the convertible. I contemplated putting up the top, but the full breeze was welcome, so I left it down. I pulled my hair back in a bun, and drove along the driveway to the road, then back out to the 1.

While I had a feeling that asking Brumhill outright wasn't going to produce a confession, it had served one purpose. He was rattled. And when guys were rattled, they made mistakes. That's where my surveillance came in handy.

I popped my earpiece in, then grabbed my cell and dialed Danny's number as I drove. Three rings in he answered.

"Hey, Jamie."

"Hey, what are you up to?"

"Photo shoot. I'm at the Beverly Hilton, poolside."

"Gee, rough life," I joked.

"It's a living. What's up?"

"I've got another job for you," I told him.

He groaned. "Have mercy. I'm not cut out for this acting gig."

I grinned. "I thought you played a pretty hot gay guy, myself."

"I'm not sure if I should be offended or enjoy the fact you just called me hot."

"Don't worry, what I need is surveillance. I'm staking out a—"

I froze mid-sentence as the passenger side window of my car suddenly shattered, glass flying onto the seat.

I screamed, instinctually ducking. The wheel swerved in my hand, sending the car into a zigzag pattern on the road.

"Jamie? Are you okay?" I heard Danny yell.

I took a deep breath, righting the wheel just in time to

avoid an oncoming car.

"Yeah, I'm…I'm fine." I glanced in the rearview mirror. Behind me was a black car, sedan, average looking. No plates.

A deafening pop sounded, causing me to jump, and something whooshed by my ear, exploding into my windshield. More glass shattered.

"Jamie, what's going on?"

What was going on was that someone was shooting at me.

I darted and weaved down Highway 1, trying to not get hit as I attempted to put the top on the car up. With it down, I was a sitting duck. The hydraulics screamed. The wind tore at the fabric. It stopped midway, so all I could make out in the rearview was blackness. I glanced down at the speedometer. Eighty-three-ish. At this speed, with the turn ahead, I'd likely end up in the ocean if a bullet didn't take out a tire first. Or my head.

A metallic taste entered my mouth. Blood. I must've bitten my lip. *Please let that be the only bleeding I do today.*

"Jamie?!"

I eased off the gas and managed the turn, just as another shot fired.

It had to be Brumhill. Who else? I'd known I'd rattled him, but I hadn't expected him to make his move this quickly. Part of me was thrilled—his bullets were leaving evidence of an attempted murder all over my car. Of course the other part of me, the one that wanted to live through this moment, was a little less happy at the number of bullets.

Another bullet pinged off my rear bumper. I sped into oncoming traffic. Horns blared. Brakes screeched. A couple of vehicles swerved onto the shoulder.

"Dammit, Jamie, answer me!" I heard Danny yell.

As I jumped the shoulder, my hands flying off the steering wheel. I may have even squeezed my eyes shut for a second, because everything turned black. When I opened them, I was careening toward Tito's Crab Shack. I barely missed sideswiping a jag parked in the lot before my tires screeched to a halt. I blinked, watching the sedan speed past me on the road.

"Danny," I said, my voice shaky and sounding nothing like my own.

"Jamie! You alright? What's going on there?"
"Call 911. Someone just tried to kill me."

# CHAPTER EIGHTEEN

––––––

By the time my heartbeat returned to normal speed, two cruisers and Sam's Cherokee were in the parking lot. After I'd reassured Danny at least a dozen times that I did not need him to come rushing out from the Beverly Hilton to play my white knight, he'd insisted on calling Sam. And while I didn't necessarily want to drag her into this, the thought of having a friendly face among the officers was too tempting to pass up. Besides, I had a feeling if I refused, Danny would have ignored my protests and come charging out himself anyway. And I couldn't deal with the testosterone at the moment.

Sam sat beside me on the curb by the Crab Shack's doors and handed me another bottle of water. I'd downed the first one, only to puke it up three seconds later in a nearby trash can. My nerves were shot, and I was sweating.

"Only a few sips. You don't want to shock your system again."

I did as instructed and watched the police officers inspect my car. They pointed to and stared at each of three bullets holes, never touching them, while waiting for their crime lab techs. Three holes! It would cost a near fortune to fill them in, and for a new paint job. Not to mention the damage I'd done while trying to put up the top at eighty miles per hour. No matter how well the agency was doing, this wasn't a part of my budget.

As I contemplated the fate of my poor roadster, I saw a black SUV turn into the parking lot.

I held my breath. Crap. It was Aiden.

He was the last person I needed here right now, picking and prodding through the events. I had hoped to give my statement to a nice anonymous detective, who would then head back up the 1 with a shiny pair of handcuffs for Brumhill and arrest him for attempted murder. I had hoped to *avoid* having to tell anyone else that I'd basically been bait to get that arrest.

Aiden parked along the side of the lot and stepped out quickly. But then he just stood there for a second and took in the scene.

I tried to not notice how good he looked in faded jeans and a light button-down shirt. He looked like he'd been interrupted in a rare casual moment. I wondered what off-duty activity my 911 had pulled him away from.

Aiden's sneakers made soft slapping sounds against the pavement. They were muffled by the police scanner, traffic, and chatter of those in the area, but I heard each one. Clear and precise. He walked over to the officers, but his eyes went to me as one of the responding officers filled him in on what happened. The officer even pointed to the trash can where my breakfast had landed. Oh, my God, how embarrassing.

"How are you feeling?" Sam stared at the bottle in my hands.

I glanced down and realized the water was gently sloshing from side to side. I was shaking. "Better." I gave a light chuckle.

Aiden stepped forward, headed straight for me, using his courtroom expression—unreadable.

My stomach churned.

He squatted before me and took my hand in his. His grip was warm and tender. His eyes were bloodshot and there were circles under them. Was he not sleeping? Did it have anything to do with me? Good.

He smiled. It was warm and made my insides instantly melt. He rubbed his thumb along the inside of my wrist. "Are you okay?"

My shaking stopped, and I suddenly wanted to throw myself into his arms and burst into tears. I refrained though. Barely.

I took a deep, cleansing breath instead. "Yes."

"Good." He smiled again. Reassuring. Confident.

He looked to Sam and asked, "When did you get here?"

"Danny called me right away."

It might have been my imagination, but I thought I saw Aiden tense a little at the mention of Danny's name. While their paths didn't cross often, there was an unspoken mutual distrust between the two. Danny thought Aiden was too squeaky clean, and Aiden was pretty sure Danny had a little dirt in his past. Both were probably right.

Aiden turned to me. "Can you tell me everything that happened? Start at the beginning."

Sam glanced at her watch.

Aiden noticed. "Do you need to be somewhere?"

Sam shook her head. "Julio's getting out of school, but I can have my mom pick him up."

"Go. I'll make sure Jamie gets home safely."

Sam shot me a tentative look.

I nodded. "I'll be fine."

"You're sure?"

I leaned over and wrapped my arms around her neck, giving her a gentle squeeze. "Thank you."

"Okay, Julio has a sleepover tonight, so if you need me later, just call." She stood and stared down at Aiden. "Take care of my girl." It came out as a demand.

He smirked. "Yes, ma'am."

She waved then hurried to her car.

Aiden stood and held out his hand. "Let's go to my car. It has A/C, and the seats aren't made of cement."

I hesitated, then placed my hand in his and allowed him to help me to my feet. Inside his vehicle, I silently thanked the heavens. Just as he promised, the seats were plush, and the interior was considerably cooler. He turned the ignition and put the air on low. Then he turned toward me and asked me to tell everything.

Maybe it was the A/C, maybe the adrenalin still coursing through my system, or maybe just the way his eyes looked so affectionate and sincere. But I did, spilling everything. I started with today's events, but backtracked all the way to the first day when he told me about Brady's gun a week ago. Had it really been only a week? It seemed my life had gotten out of control in too short a period of time.

When I was done, he let out a long breath of air, as if

he'd been holding it. "This is not good, Jamie."

"No kidding."

"I'm not joking." And the stern tone in his voice told me he really wasn't. "You could've been killed. What the hell were you thinking confronting Brumhill like that?"

"You think he shot at me?" I asked, hoping he ran with that train of thought.

Aiden shook his head. "No. I don't believe our ex-mayor took three pot-shots at you on the 1." He sighed. "But, it's possible he had someone else do it."

My mind immediately went to the friendly gardeners. Maybe they weren't so friendly after all. "So what do we do now?"

"*We* don't do anything," he told me. "You go home and rest. I wait for CSU to bring me something tangible that I can connect back to Brumhill. Until then, there's nothing I can do to keep you safe." His voice tightened on that last word.

While the sentiment had tears backing up in my throat, I shoved them down, putting on my Big Girl face. "It's okay. I can keep myself safe."

He cocked an eyebrow at me.

"Okay, I didn't do a spectacular job of that today, but I'm in one piece, see?"

A hint of a smile played at his lips. "I'm serious, Jamie."

I rolled my eyes. "Again with this serious thing. Why does everything have to be so serious with you?"

The smile died. He knew I wasn't just talking about today.

"Look," I quickly covered, "I'm not some damsel in distress. I'm a licensed PI. I carry a gun. I know how to use it. I can take care of myself."

"Fine," he said, the half smile returning. "I just can't stand the idea of you getting hurt." He rubbed the back of his hand against my cheek. "So be careful."

I smiled. "I will."

\* \* \*

After the police let me go, Aiden drove me to the office

so I could get him the flash drive and pictures I'd swiped from Derek. If they could help lead a straight line to Brumhill, I knew Aiden would follow it. When I arrived, Caleigh and Maya pounced on me.

"Are you alright?" Caleigh said.

I frowned. "News travels fast," I mumbled.

"Sam told me. I'm sorry I wasn't available. I had—was busy."

I patted her shoulder. "I'm fine. Really. Do we have any coffee?" I could use a major shot of caffeine.

Maya grabbed her purse and ran around her desk. "I'll make a quick run. I hadn't heard anything until Caleigh came in, and I'd already told Mr. Fleming he could stop by. Do you want me to call him and reschedule?"

"No. It's fine."

"Okay, I'll be right back." She ran out.

I led Aiden into my office and unlocked the bottom left drawer, handing over the evidence. "Derek says he has more copies somewhere. You'll have to ask him."

"I will. You think he'll cooperate?"

I shrugged. "You never know with Derek. He finally came clean to me last night."

"Okay." He paused. "You sure you're alright?" Worry dug into the corners of his mouth.

"Yes. I am now. Thank you."

We stared at one another for a few seconds that felt like hours. Then he said a quick good-bye and left.

Caleigh immediately ran into my office. "So, fill me in. That old kook tried to kill you?"

I assumed she was referring to Brumhill. "I'm not sure, but that's my guess. Unless I suddenly looked like a deer. Driving a red sports car."

I sat at my desk and opened my laptop. In its reflection I noticed the crazy disarray of my hair. "Great. I look like hell."

She waved a hand. "Not that bad."

I gave her a hard stare then patted the left side of my hair with my hand. She was totally lying.

"Hold on." Caleigh ran out then came back with a brush and a bottle of hairspray. "So spill."

I repeated my eventful afternoon and she was my most captive audience yet—oohing and ahhing at the appropriate moments. It was rather comical. Leave it to Caleigh to help me take the edge off.

Maya rushed in with four Styrofoam cups in a tray. "What'd I miss?" she asked handing me a heavenly caramel macchiato.

"Hello?" A male voice said from the lobby.

Maya shoved the drinks at Caleigh and left to greet our guest. "Mr. Fleming, hello," I heard from the lobby

Caleigh grabbed her coffee and winked, stepping toward the door. "I'll fill her in. We'll be out there if you need us."

As she walked out, Craig stepped in. He looked flushed and delighted, wearing a huge smile across his face. His eyes were bloodshot, as if he'd been crying. I imagined they'd been happy tears.

"So, you've spoken to Phillip."

He laid both hands over his heart. "About the fact that we're going to be parents? You already know?"

"Yes, we learned about it this afternoon."

He squealed. "Isn't it the most wonderful news? I've always wanted to be a father. Before I met Phillip, I even looked into surrogates. But Philip was so young, I figured…well, I never thought he shared my desire for a family, too."

"Well, I'm very happy for you."

"Thank you. I never should have doubted him."

"It's perfectly understandable." From the corner of my eye, I spotted Danny hovering near the door. I hadn't heard the girls greet him.

Craig held out his hand. "Thank you so much."

I placed my hand in his and pumped my arm. The shake faltered mid-step.

Lines creased between his brows. "There wasn't anything else, right?"

"No. He's perfectly faithful. We had one of our best men test him."

Craig thanked me again and went up front to settle payment with Maya.

I flipped back the lid on my cup and took a long drink of

my coffee. "Are you just going to stand there?"

Danny stepped into the room. "Best man, huh? I'm the only man."

"And you're the best."

He grinned. Then his expression immediately turned serious. "You okay?"

As much as the concern around me was touching, I was getting a little tired of answering that question. "I'm fine. Really."

He shook his head. "Damn, you scared the crap out of me, Jamie. I thought for sure—"

"James!" A booming voice came from the lobby, interrupting that thought.

I flinched.

Derek.

Fab.

He filled my doorframe like a bull, looking larger and stockier than normal. "What the hell were you thinking?"

I shot Danny a death look. "You called Derek?"

Wisely, he didn't answer, instead sidestepping Derek and slipping out of the room.

Derek slammed the door shut behind him. "Brumhill tried to kill my daughter? Shooting me wasn't enough, now he's going after my baby?" he boomed.

"Shh!" I told him. Though if it wasn't for his flared nostrils and new eggplant-infused complexion, making it look like his head might pop off at any moment, it could've been a rather touching moment. He still thought of me as his baby.

"I filled Aiden in on everything. I gave him the video." That I stole from your boat. "He's processing my car, and once the evidence connects all of the dots, he'll prosecute. That's it. We're done."

Derek shot me a hard look. "You really believe that?"

"That Aiden will prosecute? Yes."

"With what?" Derek leaned in. "All we have is a guy handing the mayor a stack of money. Could be a campaign contribution. Could be he was paying off a loan. Could be a million different things that Brumhill has spent the last three years covering up. You really think there's anything that Aiden's going to find now?"

Put like that? No. "He shot at me today, Derek. On the 1. There's no way he didn't leave evidence behind."

"If *he* did it."

I paused. "He was behind it."

"He's been behind a lot of things. I haven't seen him in a courtroom yet, have you?"

Derek's words about Brumhill greasing the wheels of the court system came back to me. Was it possible he still had friends in high enough places to slip through the cracks on this one, too?

"If Brumhill knows that the authorities now have everything that you did, you're no longer a threat to him. The target's off our backs," I argued, even though it came out with less conviction than I'd hoped.

"This isn't over, Jamie," Derek said, rising from the chair. "I thought I could bury it, but I was wrong. It's not going to be over until Brumhill gets a taste of his own medicine."

"What do you mean?" I asked. I didn't like the look on his face. It was hard, dark, and as unreadable as the one he'd given me when I'd first confronted him about Brady.

"I gotta go," he mumbled.

"Derek?"

But he didn't answer me. Instead, he threw the door to my office open and stalked across the lobby.

"Derek!"

He ignored me, pushing through the glass doors and disappearing down the hallway.

I bit my lip as Maya and Danny stood by.

"Everything okay?" Danny asked.

I shook my head. "I don't know. He…" I trailed off, gesturing after Derek.

How stupid would he be? Stupid enough to take matters into his own hands? To go after Brumhill himself?

I closed my eyes and thought a really bad word. Of course he was! This was Derek we were talking about.

"Danny!" I called, popping my eyes open.

"Yeah?" He was at my side in an instant.

"I need your van."

"What's going on?" he asked, concern lacing his expression.

"I think my dad's going to shoot Brumhill."

# CHAPTER NINETEEN

———

We lost Derek along the freeway, but it didn't matter much as I already had a pretty clear idea where he was going.

"You really think he'll kill the guy?" Danny asked as he hung a sharp left onto the exit.

It was all I'd thought about on the ride over. I had no clue. Derek was from a different generation of PI's, one that was inherently wary of the police. And, I supposed if Brady had been my drinking buddy, I might agree with good reason. But whether or not Brumhill ever saw the inside of a courtroom over the video Derek had taken, it was unlikely he could make another move for the rest of his life without the DA's office watching him.

Not that Derek felt any justice in that.

Danny pulled his van through the gates and up the front drive of Brumhill's estate. I immediately saw Derek's Bonneville in front of the house. The driver side door was open, the keys dangling in the ignition.

The air was still. Not a sound, not a bird. My first thought was that it was the calm before the storm.

Then the storm hit.

A gunshot echoed from inside the house, followed by a shattering sound.

I raced up the steps, Danny a beat behind me, and pushed open the door. Derek stood in a room directly to the right of the entrance, next to an old-fashioned loveseat on swirly, thin legs. Brumhill stood across the room from him, by a stone fireplace. No one was bleeding, but shards of glass were scattered by Brumhill's feet. He looked bewildered, staring down at the broken vase, a small puddle of water, and a handful of dying tulips.

"Next time I aim for your nads, Brumhill. Admit you shot at my daughter." Derek's voice was direct and commanding. And the gun in his hand, pointed at said nads, only added to his menacing air.

"Are you fucking crazy? You can't enter my home and wave a gun around. You're going to jail for this, Bond."

"Not if I kill you first."

"Derek. Stop."

Derek threw only a cursory glance my way, his attention never leaving Brumhill. "Stay out of this James."

Brumhill, on the other hand, looked infinitely glad for the interruption. "You named your daughter James?" he chuckled, but there was no laughter in his eyes. He was stalling. He knew as well as I did that the look on Derek's face was deadly serious.

"Admit what you did, Brumhill."

"I've done nothing. I have no idea what you're talking about, you crazy old drunk."

Personally, I didn't think Derek looked drunk. He looked scary sharp. If I were Brumhill, I'd be stalling too.

Danny took a step toward Derek, edging around the back of him, his eyes squarely on the gun. Though neither Derek nor Brumhill seemed to pay attention to either of us. They were locked in a silent sparring match, eyes intent on each other, waiting for the other to flinch first.

I took a step back, feeling under my blazer for my Glock 27. Though who I planned to point it at, I wasn't sure. It wasn't like I was going to shoot Derek.

"It was you that hit my daughter's car today, Brumhill, and you that hit me three years ago."

"You're delusional. I was here all afternoon."

"Sure you were. You never get your own hands dirty."

"Which is why you'll never pin anything on me."

I pulled my gun from its holster, my hands loose on the trigger, ready to spring as I watched Danny close in on the old man.

Derek glanced his way briefly, but I could tell there was little short of a bomb going off that would deter him at this point. "The Assistant District Attorney knows all about you, Brumhill,"

Derek told him. "He has evidence of you taking money from Campbell. Think he'll sing now?"

Brumhill narrowed his eyes. "If he lives. Prison is a dangerous place."

Derek growled, and took a step toward Brumhill.

"Derek, put the weapon down," Danny said, moving closer as well.

Derek practically rolled his eyes. "Stay out of it, Flynn," he ground out.

"You've got nothing on me," Brumhill said, taking a small step backward. Though I noticed his voice wavered. "And if you really think a coerced confession at gunpoint is going to stick, you're dumber than you look, Bond."

"I'm not looking for a confession," Derek said, his voice hard. "I'm looking for justice."

"Dad, please, put the gun down," I pleaded, my voice as low and calm as I could make it given the circumstances.

"Yeah. Listen to *James*," Brumhill said, adding emphasis to my name. Then he picked up a photo frame and threw it like a boomerang at my head.

Me! Not the man with the gun.

I didn't have time to react. It clocked me in the temple. Pain flashed through my head and down my neck. Derek's eyes cut to me. Danny took the opportunity to pounce, lunging at the gun in Derek's hand. That was all I saw before I staggered and fell on my butt.

It took me a minute to refocus. My Glock had been knocked from my hands, skidding across the floor. I heard loud, scuffling footsteps and a string of curses that would make a sailor blush. When I got my bearings again, Derek was on his knees, searching under the loveseat. He must've dropped his gun when Danny hit him. Danny was on the floor too, on the other side of the loveseat, trying to find the gun first. Brumhill was bent over one of those old-timey desks with the roll top, opening drawers. I watched in horror as he slammed one shut, then turned, holding a pistol in his right hand.

Was there anyone in L.A. who didn't own a weapon?

"Watch out," I screamed and struggled to my feet.

Time seemed to slow down just so I could watch the

events unfold.

Derek and Danny looked up as one to see Brumhill moving toward Derek, gun first.

Defenseless, Derek's expression flipped from shock to fear.

Danny, with one hand still beneath the sofa, got to his knees. As he rose, I noticed Derek's gun in his hand. He turned it on Brumhill.

But Brumhill was only focused on Derek, a victorious smirk contouring his features. He didn't hesitate, didn't flinch, but wrapped his finger around the trigger and pulled.

Danny dove toward Derek, firing in Brumhill's direction.

Shots filled the air, and I heard screaming erupt from my throat.

A bullet hit Brumhill, making his body twist and fall backward onto the desk. Danny collapsed onto Derek.

I gulped in air, the smell of gunfire stinging the back of my throat. Brumhill wasn't moving. Danny lay across Derek's legs. His grip had loosened, and the gun fallen to the floor. A dark red stain spread across his left shoulder.

I blinked, not able to process what I was seeing.

Derek moved with lightning speed, pulling off his shirt, bunching it into a ball, and pressing it against Danny's wound.

Danny grunted. His eyes were stuck at half-mast.

I stifled a cry.

"You'll be fine, Flynn" Derek said, then looked at me. "Get Brumhill's gun away from him. Be careful."

I walked around the sofa to the desk. Brumhill had slumped to the floor, on his stomach. The gun was above his head. I kicked it into the middle of the room, then exercised all my arm muscles to flip the heavy man over.

Danny's bullet had struck him square in the chest.

I checked for a pulse in his neck.

Nothing.

\* \* \*

Derek and I walked into hospital room number two-thirty-six holding a small bouquet of daisies and a fifth of scotch.

The liquor was Derek's idea. The daisies were mine.

Danny was in the bed closest to the door. The cloth partition to the neighboring space was partially closed, but I could see the other bed was empty. The TV facing Danny played the news.

When he saw us, he pushed the mute button on his remote, and greeted me with a lopsided smile that sent a rush of familiar warmth flooding through me. It was a smile I'd taken for granted, but had spent a good part of the night worrying that I'd never see again. Danny was always there. The thought of him suddenly not being there had shaken me more that I wanted to admit even now, hearing the steady, reassuring beeps of the monitors hooked up to his vital signs. He'd saved my father's life. The man who never liked him, always gave him crap—whether directly to his face or just to mine. Danny saved him. And I knew he'd done it for me.

"My hero," I said, leaning in to give him a peck on the cheek. While my tone was light, I hoped he knew I was only half joking. I set the flowers on his bedside table.

"Is that all it takes to get a kiss from you, Bond? A gunshot wound?"

I swatted at his good shoulder.

His hair was more tousled than usual, but other than his bandaged left shoulder, he looked like his color was good and he'd slept well. I couldn't say the same for myself, as I'd spent the night in a hard, plastic chair in the waiting room, chewing my nails while they wheeled him into surgery. The doctor had reassured us that the bullet didn't look like it had hit any major arteries, but it wasn't until Danny had been in recovery, sleeping off the effects of the anesthetic, that I'd been able to breathe a sigh of relief.

Derek hadn't sustained any injuries, and other than it being sore when I touched my head, my wound only required a Band-Aid. Brumhill, however, was definitely dead. Whether he'd be buried as a celebrated ex-mayor or a corrupt politician was yet to be determined. Derek and I had given statements to the police as soon as they'd arrived at the scene, but I could tell that our stories were way beyond the paperwork that the responding officers knew how to process. I wasn't sure what the DA's office was going to do with the whole mess, but no one had arrested Derek or Danny yet, which I took as a good sign.

Derek walked to Danny's right side and held out his hand. "I didn't get a chance to thank you yesterday. You saved my life, Flynn."

Danny looked at Derek's hand as if it might bite him any second. But he took it, gripping tightly. "My pleasure. Sir," he added.

Derek withdrew his hand and cleared his throat, the emotion in the room clearly having hit his tolerance level. "We brought you booze. Don't mix it with pain meds, kid."

Danny grinned. "Thanks. I won't."

Derek pointed to the door. "I'm going to see if I can find something edible in the cafeteria. You want anything, James?"

I shook my head. "I'll catch up to you in a bit." I paused. "And leave the candy stripers alone," I called after him.

He shot me a grin over his shoulder that said he was clearly going to ignore that advice.

"Can't teach an old dog new tricks," Danny observed with a laugh.

I shrugged. "He's an old dog, but I couldn't live without him." I sat on the edge of his bed. "Thanks."

Danny took my hand. "You're welcome, Jamie."

While it should have been uncomfortable having my best friend hold my hand in his, his thumb rubbing the back of my fingers in something akin to a caress, it suddenly felt like the most natural thing in the world. I reached out and brushed a few strands of his tussled hair from his forehead. His eyes were a pale, ocean green in this light, little flecks of blue dancing in them as he stared at me with an emotion that for once I wanted to hear him voice.

"You said there was something you wanted to talk to me about?" I prompted him.

I watched his Adam's apple bob up and down. "There was."

"Well, I'm here. No time like the present."

Danny took a deep breath, licked his lips. His face was serious, his expression open, the charming, jovial facade completely stripped away.

I felt myself leaning in.

"Jamie," he started.

But that was as far as he got before someone cleared their throat from the doorway.

I looked up to find Aiden standing there, a small frown pulling between his brows. "I'm not interrupting anything, am I?"

I quickly pulled my hand back from Danny, getting up from the bed like I was guilty of something.

The frown deepened.

"ADA Prince," Danny said, his voice deadpan. If he resented the interruption, he didn't show it.

Aiden nodded to Danny, then me. No smile, no hello. Just a tight nod.

"What? No gift?" Danny said, gesturing to our offerings on the table beside him. Clearly the facade was back, whatever emotion he'd felt a moment ago swallowed.

Aiden ignored the jibe. "Glad to see you're doing well, Mr. Flynn."

"I am." Danny's eye briefly glanced my way, as if I had something to do with his state of wellness. I looked down at my hands. Why did I suddenly feel so guilty? Like the air was charged with testosterone, all aimed at me?

"To what do I owe the pleasure of your company, Prince?" Danny asked. "Come to arrest me for shooting our good mayor?"

I could have sworn Aiden entertained the thought for a moment, not altogether hating it. "No. Actually, I came to tell you that Campbell is talking."

I perked up. "What's he saying?"

"He confessed to paying off Brumhill. You were right. We also discovered that Brumhill owned a 9mm years ago. We can't be certain it's the same one found in Brady's possession, because the numbers were filed off, but knowing that Bernstein and Brumhill were both involved with Campbell, it's not a leap to imagine he gave the gun to Bernstein."

"With instructions to kill Derek and Brady before they could show anyone the video," I added.

"We'll never know for sure who pulled the trigger on your dad, but the scenario fits the evidence," Aiden hedged.

"Then Bernstein really did go to Brady's to kill him?" Aiden's jaw tightened. "Possibly."

Which I knew put a big hole in his case against Brady.

"So, I get a free pass on this one then, Mr. ADA.?" Danny asked.

Aiden nodded. "There is no evidence to suggest that Brumhill's shooting was anything other than what you claimed: self-defense."

Danny grinned. "In fact, doesn't it make me kind of a hero, taking out a guy like that? Do I get a medal or something?"

Aiden shot him a look. "Don't press your luck. The gun you shot him with was unregistered."

I rolled my eyes. I was gonna kill Derek.

"Anyway," Aiden said, clearing his throat again, "I just thought you'd want to know." He addressed Danny, but his eyes were on me.

"Thank you," I told him.

"I'll…see you around," Aiden said, still looking my way. And if I didn't know better I'd have said there was a note of hope and a question mark at the end of that statement.

I paused. Then nodded in the affirmative. "Definitely."

Aiden gave me a small smile, then turned and walked out, his shoes clicking along the tiled floors.

"That guy is wound tighter than a top," Danny said after he left.

"Give him a break. He's under a lot of pressure."

"You've got a thing for him don't you?" Danny asked, cocking his head to the side.

I watched Aiden's back retreat down the hall. Honestly, at the moment I didn't know who I had a thing for or what kind of thing that might be. All I knew was I needed a hot shower, a long nap, and a strong cocktail. Not particularly in that order.

"You know me, Danny," I answered. "I'm a low commitment kind of girl."

Danny grinned, showing off that dimple in his left cheek. "I'll take that as a sign I still have a chance, then."

# CHAPTER TWENTY

———

I pushed through the doors of Mel's diner the following week and was immediately greeted by the scents of pancakes and French Fries. It was mid-afternoon and the place was dead, a few scattered patrons still lingering over their late lunches, but the early-bird special crowd not yet having made an appearance. I spotted Jillian wiping down a booth in the corner.

She spied me right away, gesturing to the table she'd just cleaned as she sat.

"Hi, Jillian," I said, sliding into the seat opposite.

Her eyes held bags under them and were puffy and swollen as if she'd been crying more often than not in the last few days.

"Hey. Thanks for meeting with me," she said.

"Of course."

I'll admit, I'd been surprised when she'd called yesterday, saying she was working a double and wanted to meet with me this afternoon. She said she'd kept my business card and there was something I needed to know. Of course, being the curious cat that I was, I'd immediately accept the invitation.

"I, uh, I wasn't sure if I should call you or not."

"Is everything okay?" I asked.

Her eyes darted from the door to the empty counter and back as she licked her lips. If I had to guess from their chapped state, it was a gesture she'd been indulging in a lot lately. "Yeah," she answered. Though I didn't quite believe her.

When she didn't go on, I prompted, "You said you had something you wanted to talk about?"

She nodded, clasping her hands in front of her so tightly that her knuckles went white. She took a deep breath. "He's gone."

"Brady?"

She nodded. "Took off last night."

After the evidence supporting Brady's version of events the night Bernstein died surfaced, Aiden had been forced to drop the murder charge against him. He'd made a deal with Brady's lawyers to submit to a lesser charge of being in possession of an unregistered weapon, but Brady had only been sentenced to time served. He'd been let go a free man. As much as I was sure there were plenty of things that Brady was guilty of, killing an unarmed man in cold blood was not one of them.

At least, not this time.

"Jack said he was done with this town," Jillian continued. "That we could all go to hell." Her voice cracked on the last part, and I felt a mix of sympathy and irritation with her. I'd hoped this case would open her eyes to who he really was and give her the courage to leave him. I'd never guessed it would be the other way around.

"You're better off without him," I blurted out.

She sniffed and nodded. "I know." She paused, then brought her eyes up to meet mine. "I really do," she said with more conviction this time. "It's just…hard. Our relationship is complicated."

Complicated relationships I understood.

"What was it you wanted to talk to me about?" I prompted her again. Whatever it was had been urgent enough that she'd wanted to see me right away, but now it seemed as if she was dancing around it.

She took another shaky breath. "Look, I know Jack threatened you. It was in the papers," she explained. "But he wouldn't have really hurt you."

That I doubted, but I nodded anyway, motioning for her to go on.

"He was just scared. Before he left, Jack told me everything." She paused, licked her lips again as if unsure how much to share with me. But eventually went on. "Brumhill told him that Bernstein acted on his own. When your dad showed Jack that tape, he knew Brumhill was too big of a fish to ever go to jail over it. So Jack took matters into his own hands. He threatened Brumhill and Bernstein, said if they didn't quit protecting drug dealers on his beat, he'd go after them both personally."

"I can image how that went over."

Jillian nodded. "Yeah, well, Jack always had more heart than brains. Anyway, Brumhill said it was Bernstein's idea then to take out both Jack and your dad in order to keep their arrangement quiet. Brumhill said it was Bernstein who shot your dad."

I bit my lip. It was a pretty convenient story for Brumhill to tell with Bernstein dead. But the truth was, Derek was right. We'd probably never know which of the two had pulled that trigger, or even if they'd hired Campbell or one of his gang thugs to do the deed for them. As much as it pained me to say it, my dad's shooting was one case that would never really have a pretty bow tied around it at the end.

"So then Bernstein went after Brady?" I asked.

Jillian nodded. "Only Jack was ready for him, and Bernstein ended up dead. When they arrested him, Brumhill promised that if Jack kept his mouth shut, he'd make sure that the trial was thrown. Jack would walk, and everyone would be happy. Brumhill was even paying his lawyer's fees."

Why was I not surprised to hear that the weasely Richmond had been in bed with Brumhill, too? "But if Brady talked?" I asked.

"Then Brumhill would make sure he went to prison, innocent or not." Jillian licked her lips again. "Bad things happen to cops in prison. Especially rats."

"That's why he wanted me to drop it," I said, pieces falling into place. "He was afraid that if I pressed, Brumhill might think he'd talked to me, and he'd make sure Brady went down for the murder."

Jillian nodded. "He was scared. Look, I'm not stupid. I know that Jack wasn't an angel. But he wasn't a bad guy. Once in a while he took justice into his own hands, but he never hurt anyone who didn't deserve it."

"Except you?" I couldn't help blurting out, remembering the domestic incidents Aiden had mentioned.

Jillian's cheeks went red. "Those were misunderstandings. Which is what I told that ADA guy. Jack had a temper. Sometimes he got loud and a little…scary."

I had to agree with her there.

"Do you know where Brady went?" I asked. "Where he's headed now?"

Jillian shook her head. "He said it's better if I don't. He needs to disappear." She paused, lowering her voice, eyes darting to the door again. "Because he said he's still a loose end, and they're still after him."

I froze, the hairs on the back of my neck standing up. "They?"

She didn't answer, instead staring down at her hands, her knuckles stark against her work-worn hands.

"Jillian," I softly prompted. "Who was Brumhill going to pay off to make sure that Brady's trial was thrown?" Even as I asked the question, I felt nausea settle in my stomach. There was only one way he could have pulled that off, and it was if Brumhill had someone inside the DA's office.

But Jillian didn't meet my gaze. "I don't know. Jack didn't either. But he was scared."

I had 100% faith that Aiden was not involved in anything that had to do with throwing the trial. For one thing, three years ago he was in Kansas City. He hadn't even moved to town until after Brumhill left office and couldn't possibly be in Brumhill's fold. But there were plenty of people who could be. Aiden's vigilant, dark-haired co-counsel? The District Attorney himself? Or did this go higher, all the way up to the Judge Judy look-alike presiding over the trial?

I tried to calm those hairs on my neck down and tell myself it didn't matter now. Brumhill and Bernstein were both dead, Campbell was spilling names like a sieve, and Brady had probably just spent so many days looking over his shoulder that he couldn't remember what safe felt like.

"Look, I don't know if Jack was just being paranoid or what," Jillian went on, voicing my same thoughts, "but I just…well, I just thought you should know. You know, why Jack threatened you. He never meant to hurt you or your dad. Honest."

I nodded, sure she believed that even if I still had my doubts.

"Order's up, Jill," the stocky guy in kitchen yelled through the window separating the dining room, setting a plate of eggs down on the sill.

Jillian glanced at the platter. "I gotta go." She shot a weak smile my way. "It's my last day here."

I raised an eyebrow. "Really? Good for you."

"Yeah, I've got a cousin in San Jose who says she can get me a job at a start-up." She shrugged. "It's just answering phones, but anything's better than sticking around here now. I'm so over this place."

I smiled, genuinely happy for her. She'd been through some rough times. Hey, even the best of us could have bad taste in boyfriends once in a while. I hoped her life started looking up soon.

I watched her slip out of the booth, cross the checkered floor, and grab her order, depositing it at a table near the windows where an older couple sat. I was just imagining her swapping her apron and saddle shoes for a pencil skirt and pumps in Silicon Valley e-commerce when my cell rang.

"Bond?" I answered.

"Hey, it's me," I heard Maya's voice in my ear. "A new client just came in, and she wants to meet with you this afternoon. You free?"

"What's' the case?" I asked, slipping out of the booth and stepping back into the sunshine outside.

"You're gonna love this one," Maya said, a grin in her voice. "Mother-of-the-bride wants to test her daughter's fiancé before the wedding."

I felt an answering smile hit my face as I walked to my rental car, parked at the curb, and beeped the alarm off. "Don't tell me we're crashing a bachelor party?"

"I don't have deets yet. But Caleigh is practically giddy over here," she told me. I could hear the blonde giggling in the background, shouting something to Maya. "She says she has this move where she jumps out of a cake that always kills."

I couldn't help a chuckle as I opened my door and slipped behind the wheel. "There's a great story that goes with that, isn't there?"

"One can only hope. So, should I schedule her for, say, four?"

"I'll be there," I promised before hanging up.

I flipped my sunglasses down over my eyes, turned my engine over and pulled out of the parking lot, heading east on Ventura.

The sun was shining, the clients were flooding in, and I was about to pay a girl to jump out of a cake. For a Bond, life didn't get much better than this.

# ABOUT THE AUTHORS

Gemma Halliday is the *New York Times* and *USA Today* bestselling author of the *High Heels Mysteries*, the *Hollywood Headlines Mysteries,* the *Deadly Cool* series of young adult books, as well as several other works. Gemma's books have received numerous awards, including a Golden Heart, two National Reader's Choice awards, and three RITA nominations. She currently lives in the San Francisco Bay Area where she is hard at work on several new projects.

To learn more about Gemma, visit her online at
www.GemmaHalliday.com

Jennifer Fischetto, national bestselling author, writes dead bodies for ages thirteen to six-feet-under. When not writing, she enjoys reading, eating, singing, and watching way too much TV. She also adores trees, thunderstorms, and horror movies. She lives in Western Massachusetts with her two awesome children, who love to throw new ideas her way, and two fuzzy cats, who love to get in the way.

Unbreakable Bond is her debut novel.
For more information, follow her on Twitter:
@jennfischetto or visit her at http://jenniferfischetto.com.